PLAY SAFE

AMBER GARZA

To my brother, Matt, the real Coach Hopkins. Thank you for all your help. I couldn't have written this book without you.

EMMY

Four. That's the number of times I've caught Josh in a lie since we've been together. Once for every month of our relationship. And tonight makes five. My gaze hones in on him standing in the middle of the open field with his friends Chase and Nolan. A fire pit roars in front of them, casting an eerie orange glow on their faces. Nearby, several girls giggle incessantly like they're watching a show at a comedy club. Then they glance in Josh's direction as if trying to catch his attention. My stomach sours.

"I'll be right back," I say to my best friend Ashley.

She nods, her long bleached blond hair shimmering in the moonlight. "I'll go see if I can find a drink." I'm not surprised at her response.

1

Ashley never turns down an opportunity to party. "Holler if you need me."

After she saunters off, I stalk over brittle yellow grass, making my way toward the fire. Josh doesn't even notice me, but his friends do, and their eyes widen. I glower down my nose at them, crossing my arms. Responding to his friends' frantic and not so subtle pointing, Josh finally cranes his neck in my direction.

"Em, what are you doing here?" Josh asks, as if I'm the one who did something wrong.

At his accusing tone, I feel a little of my earlier bravado wither. The girls clustered near the fire, turn toward us, their eyes alight with curiosity. The last thing I want to do is get into a fight with Josh in front of all these people. I glance down at the beer in his hand, then up at his glazed eyes that tell me this isn't his first one. Arguing with Josh when he's drunk is never a good plan, but I can't help it. I'm angry, and I want answers. I'm tired of all the lies. Besides, why does he even want to date me if half the time he's lying in order to get out of spending time with me?

"You told me you had a baseball thing with the team tonight," I state.

"I do." Josh shrugs, glancing around. "This is it."

I nod my head toward the girls. "Are they on the team?"

Josh shakes his head, one side of his lip curling up. Then he spreads out his arms in front of him. "Hey, I can't control who's going to show up to these things." His friends chuckle like he made some hilarious joke. Or maybe they think I'm the joke. Most likely it's the latter.

"But you can control whether or not I come, right?" I snap.

When darkness flashes in Josh's eyes, I realize my mistake. "Clearly I can't." He steps closer to me. "How did you even know where I was? Are you stalking me or something?"

"Stalking you?" I laugh bitterly. "Are you forgetting my brother's on the team? I overheard him talking to Christian about this party."

Josh blinks. "But Cal's not here. He had a date or something tonight."

3

Ah, I get it. He thought he was safe because he knew Cal wasn't coming tonight. Anger rises, and along with it so does my voice. "I shouldn't have to find out from my brother where my boyfriend is. I mean, is this the kind of girl you want?" I point to the girls who are staring at Josh and I like we're a damn movie they came to watch. Seriously, they don't even pretend not to eavesdrop. At least Chase and Nolan have the decency to turn their backs and act like they're having their own conversation. "You want girls like that? Because if so, then be my guest. We can just break this whole thing off right now."

Josh puffs his chest out, his forehead crinkling. As he narrows his eyes, his lips press together into a hard line. I've seen this side of him before. There's a fire simmering just below the surface of his skin, and if I'm smart, I'll back off.

And I am smart. Really smart. In fact, I've been in honors classes since elementary school. My dad used to call me his "little genius." I always test way beyond my grade, and I always get straight A's. But that's book smarts. Street smarts are a

4

completely different thing. My brother Cal has that. He may not get the best grades, but he knows how to behave in social situations. And he can read people in a way I've never been able to.

"Josh is bad news," Cal told me after he found out Josh had asked me out. It was only a week after Josh joined the baseball team.

"You don't even know him," I argued back.

"I don't need to know him to tell what kind of guy he is," Cal responded.

But I didn't listen. Josh was the cutest, most popular boy who had ever asked me out. And I wanted to believe the best about him. Besides, he seemed like a nice guy.

And he is. Sometimes. Sort of.

"Don't challenge me." Josh's hand clamps around my upper arm. It stings, and I bite down on my lip. His mouth moves close to my ear. "You want to push me, Em. I'll push right back." He tugs me away from the fire. Away from his friends and the girls who have been watching us with rapt attention. And suddenly I long for the audience again. Josh is mad. I can feel anger radiating off of

5

him in waves. He has a short fuse, and I'm concerned that tonight I may have pushed him a little too far. Darkness envelopes us the further we walk. Finally Josh stops, his hand still on my arm. "How dare you come here and embarrass me in front of my friends."

I take a deep breath. "I'm sorry, but I don't get why you keep lying to me."

"I didn't lie to you." His tone is hard, and he doesn't bother loosening his grip at all. My whole arm feels tingly now. "I told you I was going out with my friends and I did."

"You made it sound like it was a guys only thing, but clearly it isn't."

"I don't have to explain myself to you. You're not my mom. You're my girlfriend. And honestly, after tonight, I'm not even sure I want you to be that." He drops my arm with such force, I almost fall over.

But it's his words that have the most impact. "What are you saying?"

"I'm saying I don't need this shit," he spats. "I can have any girl I want. You think I'm gonna stay with someone who's needy and whiny and can't give me any room to breathe?"

His words are like a sucker punch to the gut. I take a wobbly step backwards.

"You don't mean that," I say, hoping he'll take it back. Hoping they're nothing more than words said in anger. Words with no real meaning. The kind of thing you blurt out and then immediately regret.

"I do mean it. You're acting like a fool." He glares at me, and my lips tremble. I hug myself, running my hands up and down my arms. "I don't want to be with you every minute of every day." He snorts. "God, if you can't learn to give me some space, I don't think this is going to work out."

Desperation blooms inside of me. *What have I done?* I catch Josh's dark eyes and step toward him. Reaching out, I attempt to touch his face in order to soften him up. I remember the way he kissed me so tenderly in the parking lot after school today. The way he flashed me one of his heart-stopping smiles when I got in my car and drove off. That's the thing about Josh. He can be a jerk, but he can

7

also be incredibly charming. His charisma is unmatched. Everyone wants to be close to him. And I've gotten closer than most. Before this year, Josh went to a private school. All anyone talked about at the beginning of this school year was the hot new boy at Prairie Creek High. I think everyone was shocked that I was the one who snagged him.

So, then why the hell was I screwing that all up by acting like a needy girlfriend? Josh is right. He doesn't need this. He's entitled to a night out with his friends. Besides, it's not like he was even talking to those girls. "You're right," I say, backtracking. "Let's forget the whole thing." My fingers graze the dark stubble dusting his chin. A minute ago I was so angry with him, but now I want nothing more than to kiss his full lips, to feel his arms around me. To know that he still wants me.

He swats my hand away, and it's like a splash of ice cold water on my face. I recoil.

"Just go home. You're acting crazy. We'll talk later."

"You can't be serious." I lunge toward him, trying to grab his arm. He's been upset with me before, but normally he forgives me quickly. Sometimes I feel like I have whiplash from how fast he switches emotions.

He shoves me back. "I'm dead serious."

"Hey," a familiar voice booms from over my shoulder. "What's going on?"

Great. And I thought this night couldn't get any worse.

A warm hand lands on my arm. "You okay, Emmy?"

I gaze up into the eyes of my brother's best friend Christian. The boy who was the focal point of every fantasy of mine for most of my childhood. It wasn't until Josh and I got together that I was able to temper my attraction for Christian. Well, maybe not completely, but at least I don't think of him constantly the way I used to. Of course, it doesn't help that Christian has practically lived at my house since he and Cal met in fourth grade. It seems I can't get away from him. I cringe, wondering how much of my conversation with Josh he overheard. Christian already thinks of me as a little girl who can't take care of herself. He and Cal have made it their life's mission to protect me from all the things they think I can't handle. This is going to make everything so much worse.

"I'm fine," I lie.

"Yeah, Chris," Josh says wearing a tense smile. "I've got this handled."

"It doesn't look like you do." Christian's hand slips from my arm and he takes a giant step toward Josh. When I'm alone with Josh it's easy for me to feel like he's larger than life. Next to my tiny frame he appears bigger than he is. But Christian towers over him. Not only is Christian a year older than Josh, he's filled out in places Josh can only dream of. Muscles ripple across his chest and down his arms, his shoulders are broad, his chin and face chiseled and manly. Gone are the traces of a teenage boy. This year Christian has transformed into a man. Which I guess is inevitable. He *is* almost eighteen. "If you ever lay your hands on Emmy again, you're going to regret it. The only reason I'm not shoving my fist in your face right now is out of respect for her. But trust me, I won't be so generous next time."

Josh opens his mouth like he might say something, but then closes it swiftly. *Smart move.* I'm pretty sure Christian won't give him another chance. Josh shakes his head, throwing me a look of disgust before turning around. I assume he's going to stalk off, but he pauses, pivots, and smirks at Christian. "Hey, say hi to your mom for me."

My stomach drops. *Why the hell would he say that?*

Christian fists his hands at his sides, and steps in Josh's direction. "What did you say?"

I hold my breath, knowing that if Josh utters another word he's toast. A part of me wants to see that, but the bigger part of me wants to go home.

Josh takes a step backward, holding up his hands in surrender. "Nothin'." Then he hurries away. I would laugh if my heart didn't hurt so badly.

"What a prick," Christian mutters.

"He's just drunk. He didn't mean anything by it."

"I don't care. He shouldn't have brought

my mom into this," he growls, and I feel bad for even attempting to defend Josh. I know how close Christian is to his mom, and Josh is the last person who should be mentioning her.

"Sorry about that, but you didn't need to talk to Josh at all. I could've dealt with this on my own," I mutter sullenly as Christian turns in my direction.

He flashes an amused smile. "Yeah, I can see that."

I frown, but feel a little satisfaction in knowing that I made him smile. At least he doesn't look like he's seconds away from popping a fuse anymore.

"Hey." Christian reaches out, lightly touching my shoulder. "You all right?"

When I look up at him, I think about how many times I've dreamt of this moment. I used to lie in bed at night and conjure up all these scenarios between me and Christian. And many of them ended like this. Him sweeping in and playing hero for me. But I know this isn't a fantasy. He isn't doing this because he has this deep undying love for me. He's doing this because Cal isn't here to protect me. And when Cal's not around, Christian acts like my brother. I swear the two of them have some type of pact when it comes to me. But still, I'm grateful that he stepped in. I'm not sure I could've taken anymore of Josh's hurtful words tonight.

"I told you I'm fine." I breathe in deeply through my nose and out my mouth in an effort to steady myself. One. Two. Three breaths. That's how many it usually takes. My heartrate slows in response.

"You sure?" The corners of his eyes crinkle in concern. "Because I heard what he was saying to you, and--"

Another wave of embarrassment crashes over me. "I don't want to talk about this anymore, okay? I just want to go home." At this moment I'm regretting coming here at all. When I showed up I imagined I would find Josh, call him out on lying to me, he'd apologize and we'd end up partying together. But everything went terribly wrong.

Story of my life.

"I'll take you home." Christian runs a hand

13

over his short light brown hair. I can't help but gawk at the way his arm muscles bulge with the motion. He's the catcher for the Prairie Creek Panthers varsity team. He and my brother have been playing together for years. Him catching, my brother throwing. And every game I attend, I become mesmerized with the way Christian's arms look when he catches and throws.

"Um…no. I came with Ashley, so I should probably leave with her." Looking over Christian's shoulder, I scan the field for Ashley. The party has grown since I got here, so it takes awhile to locate her. When I do, it's clear she isn't driving me anywhere. She's standing in the middle of the field holding a red Solo cup in her hand and dancing to a beat that only she can hear. Her blond hair whips around her face as her body gyrates. Some foamy liquid sprays out of her cup and dribbles down her arm. Yep, that's my best friend all right. *Always the life of the party.*

Christian raises an eyebrow. "Looks like I'll be driving both of you home."

"It does appear that way, doesn't it?"

CHRISTIAN

Emmy hasn't said a word since we dropped off Ashley. She sits in the passenger seat, staring out the window, absentmindedly fiddling with the hem of her shirt. Her eyebrows are furrowed, and her lips curl downward. Cal constantly teases his sister about how talkative she is. He says that it's easy to tell when Emmy's upset. It's when she's quiet. As I drive through the streets of Prairie Creek under the backdrop of night, I miss Emmy's stories. I miss her laugh. I miss her smile. Sure, I've often joked about how annoying it is that she talks nonstop, but honestly I find it soothing. I've gotten used to it. Besides, it's part of who she is. This silent, sullen girl beside me isn't Emmy at all.

Anger thrashes in my veins when I think of the cruel things that asshole said to her tonight. It

15

makes me glad I decided to attend the party after all. When I found out Cal wasn't going, I figured I'd skip out too. But at the last minute I changed my mind. I didn't have anything better going on anyway. The minute I saw that loser yelling at Emmy, I knew I'd made the right choice. If Cal wasn't there to protect her, then it was my job to do it. That's the way it's always been. I have Emmy's back – for Cal's sake.

At least that's what I tell myself. But deep down I know it's more than that.

When I glance over at Emmy, her gaze is fixated upward at the stars. My lips tug at the corners. "How many so far?"

Her head snaps in my direction, and she knits her eyebrows together. "What?"

"How many stars have you counted?" I press my foot on the brake, slowing as we near a stop sign.

"Twenty-seven," she speaks softly. "How did you know that's what I was doing?"

"I know a lot about you, Emmy." She has no idea how much. I know she thinks when I look at her I only see my best friend's little sister, but she's wrong. I see so much more than that. Peering over at her, my gaze catches on the jagged scar weaving around her thumb. The memory of how she got it leaps into my mind.

Cal and I were in middle school and we were headed up to the park to throw around the baseball. Emmy begged her mom to let us take her. On the walk there, we passed a stray dog. Cal stuck out his arm to protect Emmy from it, but she brushed his hand away.

"He's not dangerous," Emmy protested, moving around her brother. She was like that. Always stubborn. Always independent.

"Emmy," Cal warned.

"Cal," she said with a smile. "It's fine." As she moved closer to the dog with her hand extended, a low growl erupted from its mouth. I stiffened. Cal leapt forward, but it was too late. The dog had chomped down on Emmy's thumb. Luckily it only grazed the skin before Emmy yanked her hand back. As Cal scared the dog away, I rushed to Emmy. She bit her lip, her face the picture of bravery. Her thumb was bleeding and looked like it hurt, but she never cried.

"I told you to leave the dog alone," Cal muttered when he returned to us.

"Sorry." Emmy lowered her gaze to her scuffed tennis shoes. A warm breeze whisked over us, causing her blond hair to lift from her shoulders.

"Just promise you'll listen to me from now on," Cal pressed.

"Okay," Emmy promised.

"Hey," I say to her now as I pull up to the curb in front of her house. Sliding my hands off the steering wheel, I angle my body toward hers. Then I reach out and gently touch her scar. "Remember when you got that?"

"How could I forget? I wear the reminder every day." Light from the streetlamp slices across Emmy's pale skin, giving the illusion that her face is glowing. She always reminds me of an angel with her light features and wide innocent blue eyes, but she looks the part even more so tonight. Except for the sadness. That's new.

And I don't like it one bit.

18

"You didn't keep your promise," I tell her.

"Huh?" Her eyebrows raise.

"To Cal. You promised you would listen to him, but you didn't. At least not when it came to Josh."

She shakes her head, giving me the exasperated look I've grown familiar with over the years. It's funny. There are times I think that Emmy enjoys the attention and protection I give her. Other times it's like she wishes I'd leave her alone.

"That's completely different," she says, her tone hard.

"How so?"

"Well, for one, I'm not a little kid anymore." She tucks an errant strand of golden hair behind her ear, exposing her slender, milky white neck. My gaze slides down her smooth skin all the way to her tight-fitting top before I can stop it. *Yeah, no crap she's not a kid anymore.* I'd have to be an idiot not to notice that. "And for two, Josh is not a stray dog."

I can't help it. I laugh.

Despite her best efforts, her lips curve

upward a little. She swats me in the arm. "Shut up."

"You're the one who made the comparison."

"It wasn't a comparison. I was saying that they're not the same."

"Ah, is that so?"

She cocks her head to the side and pins me with a glare. "Look, I know you hate Josh because of everything with your mom, but--"

"That's not true. I don't hate Josh because of that," I say honestly. "None of that was his fault. I hate him because he's an ass. But mostly I hate the way he treats you."

"Stop." She sighs loudly.

"Stop what?"

"Stop playing big brother. You already did your duty for the night." She shrugs. "It's over now. I'm safe. I'm home. No need to worry."

Her words stop me cold. "This isn't some kind of job for me. I helped you because I wanted to."

"I know." She smiles, and I wonder if I misread what she was saying earlier. "You're a good friend to Cal." I open my mouth to explain that I didn't do this for Cal, but she continues before I can. "And speaking of Cal, can you please not tell him about tonight? He's not exactly Josh's biggest fan. I don't want to make things even more strained between them." She bites her lip. "I mean, it's already awkward enough when Josh comes over and stuff…"

My chest tightens. "You're not seriously going to keep seeing him, are you?"

Her shoulders bob up and down. "I don't know. Maybe. Depends on what he wants."

"What *he* wants?" I snap. "So, let me get this straight. The guy treats you like shit in front of all his friends, and now he gets to choose if you two stay together. Seems like you should be the one holding the cards right now. Hell, the way I see it, the guy needs to come crawling back and begging you to forgive him."

"He didn't mean what he said. He was drinking. Besides, it's not like he was totally off base. I *was* acting crazy."

My mouth drops. I'm dumbfounded. "Are

21

you kidding me? The guy's a jerk, Emmy. You didn't do anything wrong."

"You weren't there the whole time," she explains. "And I don't want to get into the entire thing. It's embarrassing. But I never should've shown up tonight. It was his night with the guys, and I should've just let him have it instead of acting like a needy girlfriend."

I snort. "Do you hear yourself? It's like the dude brainwashed you or something."

Anger flashes in her irises, like a light clicking on. "Excuse me?"

"Josh should be thanking his lucky stars that a girl like you wants to be with him, not the other way around."

Emmy rolls her eyes. "Oh, please. It's not like guys were knocking down my door before he asked me out."

"That's 'cause Cal and I were guarding it."

She giggles. "Nice try."

"It's the truth." I scoot forward, lifting my hand to touch her face. The minute my skin touches hers, I'm startled. *What am I doing*? Sure,

I've daydreamed about touching Emmy, but I never planned to act on it. I need to yank my hand back, to pretend I never touched her to begin with. But not before making one thing perfectly clear. She needs to hear the words I'm about to say. "You don't know how beautiful you are, do you?"

Pink stains her cheeks. "You have to say that. It's like a big brother policy or something."

She always does this – treats me like an extension of Cal. But I'm not. I'm my own person, and my feelings for her are not brotherly. *Trust me.*

"Would you stop?" *To hell with it.* I curve my hand around her cheek. "I'm not your brother. I don't say things because I have to or because I think of you as my little sister. I say them because I mean it, okay? So stop second guessing me."

Her gaze crashes into mine. "Okay," she practically whispers.

"You're beautiful and smart, and capable and funny." My fingers slip beneath her silky hair. The strands tumble down my arm. It's better than any daydream, and now that I've gotten a taste of it, I'm not stopping now. "You need to be with a guy that makes you feel that way. A guy who treats you the way you deserve to be treated. A guy who won't take you for granted." She flutters her eyelashes and leans forward. Her lips part slightly, warm breath escaping. It does something to me. Stirs my heart in a way that's terrifying.

If you had told me a year ago that Emmy would make me feel this way I wouldn't have believed you. In fact, I might have even told you that you were ridiculous. Disgusting even. I never thought of Emmy that way. Not in the kissing or touching kind of way. That would be like incest or something. She'd always been like my little sister.

Until she wasn't.

I remember it perfectly – the day Emmy went from being Cal's gangly little sister to incredibly hot chick who I couldn't stop thinking about. It was after I returned from a three-week vacation with my mom last summer. Cal texted me the day of my return and invited me to the lake with he and Emmy. I imagined that it would be a day like so many others. We'd splash Emmy, maybe throw her in the water a couple of times. She'd giggle and chase us, and probably end up getting on our nerves at some point. But I wasn't prepared for how much she'd changed since the last time I'd seen her in a bathing suit. I mean, I saw Emmy all the time, but I guess I wasn't really looking. And I hadn't seen her in a bathing suit since the previous summer.

I'll tell you another thing. I sure wasn't expecting her to be in a bikini. In past summers she'd always worn a one piece – some weathered speedo that kept everything covered. But not this day. This day she wore a skimpy red bikini.

However, it wasn't only her body that caught my attention. It was everything. Her silky hair, her heart-shaped lips, her confidence. She'd always been pretty, but now she was hot. And the way it affected me scared me to death.

Ever since that day I've been careful around Emmy. I've kept my distance more than usual. I've tried my best to keep my thoughts pure. But now that she's sitting here all vulnerable and acting like she wants me to kiss her, it's too much. My thoughts are running wild, and there's no reigning them in. When her eyes meet mine once again, I practically groan aloud.

I can't back down from this. Not now. I should've known the minute I touched her cheek that I wouldn't be able to maintain self-control. I tilt my face, lining my lips up with hers. Giving her one last chance to back out, I pause momentarily. But she doesn't move. She barely breathes, and I realize she wants this too. This spurs me on, and I softly, tenderly, press my lips to hers. They feel like I thought they would – soft, supple, moist – and taste like fruit-scented lip-gloss. Emmy has a thing for smells. Fruity ones mainly. Stepping into her bedroom is like walking into one of those lotion shops in the mall. She constantly burns candles and reapplies scented lotions. It drives Cal nuts. And truthfully, it used to bother me too. Now I dream of it. I fantasize about her apple lotion and cherry lip-gloss. And now I know how it tastes. It's as delicious as I thought it would be.

Sliding my tongue out, I lick along the seam of her lips until she parts them. As my tongue slips into her mouth, her arms wrap around my middle. I bring my other hand up to cup her face and draw her closer. There is a desperation in the way she responds to my kiss, like she's using it to erase all the pain from the evening. And I gladly let her. I deepen the kiss, my fingers massaging into her hair, tangling into the strands. My body heats up as her hands rake up my back, as her tongue melds with mine. We don't let go. We hold tighter. And I wonder if Emmy has wanted this as badly as I have.

As our lips move in sync, it hits me that this is Emmy. This is a girl I know inside and out. I've tugged at her pigtails, chased her around the yard, and held her in my arms when she was hurt. I know every expression she makes. I know the best moments of her life, and I also know the worst.

And that makes this so much more special.

It's also the reason I have to stop it.

Frantically, I tug my lips from hers. The minute the cold air hits them, I feel the emptiness. I think of kissing her again, but resist the urge. As much as I want Emmy, I can't do this. *We* can't do this.

As if in response to my thoughts, I look

past Emmy's shoulder. And standing on the sidewalk is the reason this will never work.

"Cal," I mumble.

EMMY

"What?" I ask, certain I misheard him.

"Cal," he repeats.

Nope. I heard correctly.

"Um…no, I'm Emmy," I joke, because I have no idea what else to say. Why would my brother's name be the first thing out of Christian's mouth after kissing me? I don't even want to touch that question with a ten-foot pole.

"No, Emmy." He points his index finger behind me. "Cal is right there."

I peer over my shoulder, spotting my brother moving toward us. "Oh."

Christian's hand lights on my arm. Goosebumps arise on my flesh as the memories of his gentle touch and heart-thumping kiss flood my mind. I look up at him, and he throws me a

29

cautionary expression. "This. Never. Happened," he says firmly, punctuating each word.

My stomach tumbles to the ground. His words sting, but I'm determined not to let it show. How many times am I going to let a guy stomp on my heart tonight? "Right." I nod, and pull in a deep breath. Then I turn, grabbing the door handle.

"Emmy." Christian reaches for me, but I yank the door open and step out of the car.

"Hey, Cal." I force a smile I don't feel.

Cal's forehead furrows under the bill of his hat. Even though he had a date tonight, he's wearing standard Cal attire – jeans, a t-shirt, and his baseball cap. Actually, it's similar to what Christian is wearing, except he's not wearing his ball cap tonight. Cal glances suspiciously between me and Christian, shoving his hands deep into his pockets. I wonder if he saw us kiss. A part of me hopes he did. Then it can be out in the open. Another part of me hopes he'll never find out. I can tell Christian is hoping the latter by the panic-stricken look on his face. My stomach knots. "What's going on?" Cal asks.

"Nothing," I answer quickly. Too quickly. Christian's eyes flash. Cal's quizzical expression deepens. "Christian just gave me a ride home from the bonfire party."

"You went to the party?" The puzzled look is replaced by one of anger.

"Ashley wanted to go," I explain.

"You went with Ashley?" His face darkens. Cal doesn't like Ashley much, but he likes her more than Josh, so I know I made the right choice in mentioning her over him.

"You know how she likes to party." I shrug. A car drives past our house, its lights flickering over our bodies. A breeze whisks my hair softly, and a few pieces flutter over my face. "Anyway, she was too drunk to take me home, so Christian did."

"You weren't drinking, were you?" Cal takes a step toward me.

"No." I breathe in his face. "See."

He scrunches up his nose and waves his hand in the air. "God, Em, that's gross."

"Oh, shut up." I punch him good-naturedly in the arm. "My breath doesn't stink." *At least*

31

Christian didn't seem to be bothered by it. My gaze drifts over to Christian still sitting in the front seat. Our eyes meet, but he quickly averts his. Another chink in my heart. I've got to get out of here. "Anyway, Christian got me home safe. He did his brotherly duty for the evening so you can stop worrying about me now, Cal." I step past him. "I'm going to bed. It's been a long night."

"Good night, Emmy," Christian calls after me.

My shoulders stiffen momentarily, but I don't bother responding. At this point I'm not even sure I can. My heart feels shattered, torn into a million pieces. A few minutes ago I thought I'd finally gotten what I've always wanted. But you know the old saying – be careful what you wish for. Everything comes with a price. However, this price is a little too high. It was bad enough when I had to contend with my fantasies about Christian. I wanted him without even knowing what that meant. Now I do. I know what it feels like to have his lips against mine, to feel his arms around me. And I also know what it feels like to have him reject me, toss me aside like I'm nothing more than a dirty secret.

This. Never. Happened.

He said the words with such force, such finality. Whatever happened between us is something he regrets. And that's too much to bear. With my head down, I hurry toward the front door. My hands are slick and shaky when I reach it, and it takes longer than I'd like to get my key into the lock. I practically sigh aloud when the door opens, and I step inside. It's dark and quiet. Mom and Dad must already be in bed.

Thank god for small favors.

Sometimes Mom stays up late writing in her office, but I don't detect the sound of fingers on a keyboard. Peering around the corner, I note that her office door is closed and no light escapes underneath. I blow out a breath. The last thing I want is a heart-to-heart with her right now. Mom writes romance novels, and because of that she mistakenly thinks she's an authority on it. I've reminded her over and over that making up fictional stories is not the equivalent of being a relationships counselor. Her characters aren't real people. The reason their relationships work so well is because they're made up. But rational conversations never go well with Mom. I swear that woman not only writes about fictional worlds – she lives in one. I've gotten used to it over the years. But it was tough when I was younger and I was the only kid who was still standing outside of the elementary school hours after school ended because Mom was too taken by her latest story to remember my schedule. She can remember every line in every book she's ever written, but she can't remember when I have a minimum day. *Go figure.*

Feeling the weight of the day, I slump down the hallway toward my bedroom. My shoulders feel heavy like I'm wearing a giant coat instead of a thin jacket over my favorite pink tank top. I've almost reached my room when the front door pops open behind me. I swing around as Cal steps into the house, closing the door behind him.

"Hey," he says when he spots me. "What was going on between you and Chris?" With his thumb he points over his shoulder.

"What do you mean?" I feign confusion.

"C'mon, give me some credit. I see what's going on."

"You do?" My insides coil into tiny knots, and I struggle to catch my breath. Does he know? Am I that obvious? He comes closer, raising one brow the way he always does when he catches me doing something I'm not supposed to. Is that what's happening now? I suppose it is. I never should've allowed Christian to kiss me. Clearly he saw an opportunity. Or maybe he was just trying to prove a point. Isn't that what Cal and Christian are always doing? Trying to teach me a lesson or some crap like that? Then again, maybe it had nothing to do with me at all. Perhaps Chris was using me as a way to get to Josh. Whatever it is, it's clear his feelings for me aren't what mine are for him. Josh may be a jerk sometimes, but at least I know where I stand with him. Christian likes to think he's so much better than Josh, but what he did tonight was pretty low.

"Sure. You're getting older. More mature. And I know you think you don't need me and Chris looking out for you," he says, "but you're wrong.

You have no idea what guys are capable of, little sis."

Trust me, I do. I snort, but don't say what I'm thinking. Then he'll want an explanation, and I don't have one I'm willing to give him.

"Luckily, you have Chris and me around to protect you."

Yeah, I'm lucky all right.

He musses my hair with his hand.

"Stop."

"Make me."

"Fine." I shove his hand away, but he grabs my arm and pins it behind my back. A tiny yelp escapes through my lips. "Let go," I speak through gritted teeth.

"You know what you have to say." Cal grins.

"Oh, please. I'm not saying it."

"Then I guess you don't like your arm as much as I thought." He grips me tighter. I writhe around, trying to loosen his fingers. But it's no use. It never is. No matter how many times I struggle, he always wins.

"Okay." I exhale. "You're stronger than me. You're the greatest. You're the winner," I rattle off the words with no inflection at all.

"It doesn't sound like you mean it."

"I don't," I snap.

"Wrong answer." He doesn't let up. His fingers hold me in place.

"Cal!" The word bursts out in a frustrated grunt. "It's been a long night. I don't want to play your stupid games." I may be younger by over a year, but sometimes it feels like I'm the older one. Dad says it's because boys mature slower than girls. But I really hope Cal catches up one of these days.

"What's going on?" Dad appears in the doorway of his bedroom at the end of the hall. He's wearing a wrinkled white t-shirt and plaid pajama pants. What's left of his salt and pepper hair is sticking up all over his head.

"I was just reminding Emmy that I'm the stronger one," Cal responds proudly.

"Well, can you wait until morning to show her? We're trying to get some sleep," Dad answers dryly.

"Sure thing." Cal releases my arm and flashes dad an A-okay sign. He's such a cheeseball.

"Good night, Dad." Grateful to be free, I slip into my room and flick on the wall switch. The bright light almost blinds me.

"Get to sleep, you two." Dad's bedroom door clicks closed.

I glare at Cal. "You heard Dad. Go get some sleep."

"I'm not tired." He leans against my doorframe. "Tell me about tonight. How was the party?"

The entire night plays like a movie reel in my mind, and I suddenly feel exhausted. Perching on the edge of my bed, I rub the back of my neck. "Nothing really to tell."

"I don't buy it."

I throw up my arms. "Why don't you just say whatever it is you want to say? Clearly you're fishing for something."

"Why did Chris take you home?" He pushes off the doorframe, making his way into the room. His gaze is fixated on me, and I feel his eyes piercing my soul.

I swallow hard. "I told you. Ashley was drunk and couldn't drive me."

"The truth, Em."

He must have seen me and Christian kissing, but he's not going to say anything until we come clean. And I suppose it's better coming from me than from Christian. I gather up all my courage before opening my mouth. "Well…" I start, but Cal cuts me off.

"Why didn't Josh bring you home? Did something happen between you two?" He sits next to me, the bed creaking beneath his weight. The mattress slopes underneath me. I scoot further up onto it so I don't fall off.

Ah, so this isn't about Christian. It's about Josh. "Um…" My fingertips skate over the buttons on my jacket. One. Two. Three. Four. Five. "No. He had been drinking so he couldn't drive me either."

"Yeah, that guy never misses an opportunity to party." He chuckles bitterly, pinching the bridge of his nose.

"I seem to know someone else like that." I

elbow Cal in the side.

"Hey, I've settled down as I've gotten older."

"Ah, yes, you've mellowed out in your old age," I tease.

"Sweet of you to notice, sis." He smiles.

"You're ridiculous."

"That's not what Melissa says." He waggles his eyebrows.

"Oh, I see. So this newfound maturity is because of your older girlfriend?" Recently Cal started dating a college girl, and he likes to throw it in all of our faces constantly. As if that proves his manliness.

"Maybe." Bumping me with his shoulder, he winks.

"How was your date tonight?"

"Fun."

"That's it? Just fun?" Cal and I have always been close, but rarely does he share much with me. I sometimes wonder how different it would be if he were a girl. I imagine girls share more. I mean, I know I'm much more talkative than Cal. He reminds me of it all the time.

"It's about as much as you gave me about the party."

Two can play at this game. "Fine. You want to hear about tonight? Here goes." I lie back on my bed and take a deep breath. "Ashley came over and we were talking about what we wanted to do tonight. She wanted to go to the party. I wanted to go see that new chick flick. You know the one about the guy who goes away to school and falls in love with that super pretty girl. What's the name of the actress who plays her?" I snap my fingers. "Man, I can't remember her name. Gemma something, maybe. No, Jenna, I think. Oh, why can't I remember her name? I really like her. Do you know her name?"

Cal throws me an exasperated look. "No. But I know what movie you're talking about. It looks stupid."

"Not to me." I sit up. "I totally want to see it. But Ashley already went with Heather and Talia last week. Which was totally rude because they didn't invite me. I was kind of mad at first, but then

41

I let it go." I wave away the words with a flick of my wrist. "So I figured if we couldn't see the movie then I might as well go to the party with Ashley. But you know how Ashley is at parties. The minute we got there, she went in search of alcohol, so I went to look for Josh. When I found him he was standing in front of the fire pit with Chase and Nolan. Also, there was this weird group of girls standing off to the side giggling. You might know them. Two of them were brunette and one was blond--"

"Oh, please, make it stop." Cal leaps up, pressing his hands to his ears.

I giggle, flashing an I-told-you-so look.

"Okay, you made your point." He turns away. "Good night."

"I thought you weren't tired."

"I am now."

"You're the one who asked," I remind him.

He shakes his head and heads out into the hall. "I won't make that mistake again."

Mistake. The word rings in my head, over and over like a song on replay. I ponder the mistakes I made tonight, starting with crashing that stupid party and ending with kissing Christian. What hurts is that the last thing shouldn't be a mistake. It should be the beginning of something special. But clearly Christian doesn't see it that way. He sees it as something we need to keep secret. Something he obviously wishes never happened. I'd like to see it that same way too, but I don't. As hard as I try to tell myself it was a mistake, I know that deep down I want it to happen again.

****

I have no idea how Ashley manages to show up at my house at eight-thirty Saturday morning looking like she's ready to step onto the runway after being so drunk she could hardly stand less than eight hours before. Sure she acts like she threw herself together, stating that her hair is in a bun and she's wearing sweats. But I know from experience that Ashley spends a lot of time getting the perfect messy bun. And I'm not sure that her pink Juicy Couture sweatpants and tight sequined shirt can be categorized as lounge wear. I, on the other hand, look like I'm the one hungover with my wrinkled, torn shirt and stained flannel pants. Not to mention that my hair is knotted and matted to my head. Longingly I stare at Ashley's perfect bun, and wonder why I can never get mine to look like that. She flutters her lashes. Even though they're void of mascara, they somehow still look thick and black. Yawning, I move away from the door and allow her to enter the house. My parents must have already taken off. They'd mentioned yesterday that they had plans all day today. I can't remember what. I'm guessing Cal is still asleep since he never answered Ashley's incessant knocking, and his door is shut.

"Come in," I say groggily.

"Someone's grouchy," she says in her high-pitched voice.

I wince. It's a little early for Ashley's tone. "I'm surprised you're not." As I close the door, I marvel at how well Ashley holds her liquor. I never drink. Cal and my parents have warned me against it so much that I've never had the desire. But if I did, I'm sure I wouldn't handle it the same way as

Ashley. I haven't seen very many people who can keep up with her.

"Oh, I'm fine." She shakes her head. "I didn't have that much to drink."

As I guide her into the kitchen, I remember her sprawled out in the backseat of Christian's car singing some song I didn't recognize. "Yeah, okay," I say sarcastically.

"Oh, shut up, little Miss Stick in the Mud."

"All right, Miss Drunk off her Ass."

"Hey," she feigns offense, but then giggles.

"You're just lucky your parents were out of town."

"If not, I would've just had to crash here," she points out. "Anyway, that's why I came by. I need you to take me to pick up my car."

"How did you get here?" I ask, confused.

"Walked, silly. You're not that far."

Ugh. She already went for a walk this morning. I'm exhausted just thinking about it. "Let me just grab some coffee and change, and then I'll take you." My gaze lands on the coffee maker, and I smile. Thank god Mom and Dad made coffee before they left. The dark, aromatic liquid practically calls my name. I open the cabinet above the coffee maker and yank out a mug. "Want some?" I ask Ashley.

"No thanks. I already had some."

Seriously, how long has she been awake? I would still be sleeping blissfully in my bed if she hadn't shown up. Thinking about it makes me long for my fluffy pillow and warm comforter. After pouring myself a cup and adding a generous helping of creamer, I turn toward Ashley and lean my back against the tile counter.

"So, are you ever planning on telling me about what happened last night?" she asks sourly.

"What are you talking about?" I spin around, my heart stopping.

"C'mon, don't play dumb. I know everything already."

My lips buzz, the memory of Christian's kiss coming alive. "From who?"

Her eyes widen. "From everyone. My phone's been blowing up all morning."

"Everyone?" Furrowing my brows, I glance

down at my bare feet. My dark blue polish is chipping at the corners, and I curl them under so Ashley won't notice. *How did everyone find out?*

"Yeah, and I can't believe you didn't call me. I can't believe I had to find out from other people. I mean, this is big. Really big. Like huge."

I inhale sharply and nod. "It is. You're right." But I have no idea how she understands the magnitude of it. I've always kept my crush on Christian to myself.

"C'mere." With a look of concern, she steps forward and draws me into a fierce hug. When my head collides with her chest, I catch a whiff of her floral perfume, and it's a stark reminder that I've yet to even brush my teeth. I pull back and press my lips tightly together. "I just can't believe you and Josh broke up."

I freeze. "We what?"

"You broke up," she repeats slowly, staring at me warily. "Didn't you?"

My momentary relief that she doesn't know about Christian and my kiss is replaced by anger. "Well, I wasn't exactly sure how we left things. I

47

mean, we got in a fight, and he kind of eluded to not wanting to be together, but he never actually said the words."

"Are you okay?" She asks.

No, I'm not. But I also don't think it has anything to do with Josh. The truth is, I'm more upset about the rejection from Christian than from Josh. However, I'm pretty pissed that Josh has already spread it around that we broke up. He told other people before he even told me. *Jerk.*

"Hello." Ashley waves her perfectly manicured fingers in front of my face. "Earth to Emmy."

Snapping out of it, I take a sip of my coffee. It's a little hot and it scalds the tip of my tongue, but it seems fitting. I've been burned so many times this weekend I've lost count. "Sorry. I'm just not sure what I feel. I mean, I guess I'm confused."

Ashley hops up into one of the barstools in front of the kitchen counter. "Okay, tell me everything that happened last night."

I know she's talking about what happened between Josh and me, but as I slide into the barstool next to hers, I can't help but think about Christian. Never before have I been kissed like that. I always thought Josh was a good kisser, but I never had much to compare it to. Before dating Josh I'd only had one other kiss. It was with Miles Henry at the eighth grade dance, and it was a disaster. A slobbering, messy disaster. With Josh it was sometimes sloppy, but not disastrous. Still, I never knew a kiss could be like the one I experienced last night. I'm not sure what made it so great. Maybe it's simply the fact that I've wanted it to happen for so long. But whatever the reason, I need to stop thinking about it. Christian made it clear that it will never happen again, so there's no use replaying it. Besides, there's no way to think about it without remembering the way it ended, and that's too painful right now. Wrapping my hands around the ceramic coffee mug, I recount the events at the party. I stop when I get to the part where Christian showed up.

Ashley cringes. "Yikes. That's harsh."

"Yeah," I agree.

"But you're right. Josh never actually broke

up with you."

I sigh. "Not that it matters. Clearly it's what he wants if he's telling everyone."

"I don't think it was him. I think it was his friends."

"Still. They weren't with us when we had our fight, so he had to be the one to say something."

Ashley bites her lip, her forehead scrunching as she mulls over my words. From behind her back, Cal shuffles into the kitchen, his head down. His hair looks about like mine, and he's wearing nothing but his boxers. I clear my throat loudly, but it's too late. Ashley has already turned around and spotted him. Her gaze travels up and down his body, her eyebrows raising.

"Well, good morning there, sleepy head," she says.

He groans. "What are you doing here?"

Ashley giggles as if Cal's teasing is meant in a friendly way. And that's because she truly believes it is. Cal is sort of known for being sarcastic with his friends. But I can tell the difference between "sarcastic Cal" and "annoyed Cal". Ashley clearly cannot. She thinks Cal's constant teasing of her is because he likes her. But it's really because he doesn't.

Cal's dislike of Ashley is funny to me, because Cal is actually the reason the two of us became friends. I'd known of Ashley since middle school. Everyone did. She was the most popular girl in our school. Since I was sort of a book nerd, our paths never crossed. We had a couple of classes together, but I doubt she even noticed me. I kept to myself a lot back then.

But then at the end of last year we both attended one of Cal's baseball games. Ashley was dating one of the guys on the team, so she'd come to watch him. I can't remember now who it was. She's been through many boyfriends since then. Ashley changes guys as often as other people change socks. That day Ashley ended up sitting next to me on the bleachers, and we struck up a conversation. I was surprised by how much she knew about baseball. Hanging out with Cal and Christian had forced me to learn the game, but rarely did I meet other girls who knew it that well. The more we talked, the more we liked each other. I realized she wasn't the stuck up snob I'd always assumed she was, and she realized I was cooler than she had anticipated. And pretty soon we were besties.

"I came to console my best friend," she says.

Inwardly I groan. Why does she always have to open her big mouth?

"Console her?" Cal's eyebrows shoot up. "What's going on?"

"Nothing," I say firmly, throwing Ashley a cautionary look.

She catches it and presses her lips together, finally shutting up. Unfortunately, it's a little too late.

"Ashley?" Cal leans over the counter, pinning her with a stare. "What's going on?"

She appears close to crumbling, so I rush to explain. "Josh and I got in a little fight last night. It's no big deal."

Cal pushes himself off the counter. "I knew

something happened last night."

My face heats up. *Yeah, a lot happened last night.*

"Do you need me to kick his ass?"

He'd love that, wouldn't he? I slug Cal in the arm. "No."

"It sounds like a good offer. I might take him up on it," Ashley chimes in.

"That bad, huh?" Cal's gaze sweeps over me. "Tell me what happened, Em."

"I told you it was nothing." My ring tone floats down the hallway from my room. My head bobs up. "Hold on." Before leaving the room, I point my index finger at Cal. "No beating anyone up. I'll be right back."

"Ashley may get on my nerves, but I'd never hit a girl," Cal quips.

Ashley sticks her tongue out at him. "Very funny."

"Whatever." I shake my head and race down the hallway. When I reach my room, I head to my dresser where my cell sits on top. Josh's picture stares back at me from the screen. My heart pounds in my chest. Why is he calling? To break it off officially? While I'm having my mini freak-out session, the phone ceases ringing. The silence reverberates through my body. I stand perfectly still, wondering what my next move is. Do I call him back or freeze him out? What would a non-needy girlfriend do?

The phone vibrates and a text appears. I pick it up and read it.

Josh: I'm sorry about last night. I was drunk and stupid. Don't ignore me.

As I'm reading it, another one comes through.

Josh: Please?

"Who is it?" Ashley materializes in my doorway.

I flinch.

She flicks her gaze over her shoulder. "Sorry. I didn't mean to scare you, but I had to get outta there. Your brother was totally irritating me."

"It's okay. Come in." I wave her inside, and then flash the phone in her direction. "What should I do?"

Her eyes widen as she reads over it. "Text him back."

"Really? Even after he was such a jerk?"

Ashley cocks her head to the side and purses her lips. "Look, Em, Josh has no shortage of girls that want to be with him," she speaks in a condescending tone as if I've suddenly morphed into a kindergartener. "Last night girls were already plotting how to get him now that you two were finished. But clearly he doesn't want them. He wants you. That's huge. Most girls would kill to be in your position. You can't turn it down. Besides, it would be social suicide."

Social status has never meant as much to me as it does to Ashley. But still it does mean something. I don't want to go back to being the invisible nerd girl I was in middle school. My friendship with Ashley has opened so many doors for me. But being with Josh has elevated me to a level I never even thought possible. I know it probably sounds shallow, but that poor girl who was bullied and picked on really likes the way people treat her now. Plus, what other option do I have? If we break up, I'll end up spending all my time pining over a guy who doesn't even want me. Christian made it clear where we stand last night. And now Josh wants me back.

Ashley's right.

I know what I have to do.

Lifting my phone I type swiftly with my thumbs.

Me: I'm sorry too. Why don't we just forget the whole thing and move on?

After pressing send, I hold my breath while waiting for him to respond.

Josh: Ok.

Me: We're good then?

Josh: We're good.

It's not exactly a declaration of undying love, but it doesn't seem like anyone's handing those out lately. I glance up at Ashley.

"You can tell everyone that Josh and I are not broken up."

She squeals and throws her arms around my neck. "Oh, this is so great."

It hits me that I should be the one excited,

not Ashley. So then, how come I'm not?

CHRISTIAN

A few minutes ago it was light out, but now it's dark. It's as if someone closed a curtain around the sun. Grey clouds move overhead, and I wonder if it will rain. Usually I would pray for the rain to hold off until after practice, but today I'm sort of hoping for a downpour. I'm not feeling it. Partly because I helped Mom at the antique store all day yesterday. She had me hauling boxes and lifting crap for hours, so now my arms are sore.

But that's not the entire reason. Truth is, I'm used to assisting Mom. I spend many weekends and afternoons at her shop. I have for years. Mom runs Prairie Creek Antiques by herself, and since I'm pretty much the only guy in her life, I'm the go-to person for most of the lifting and stuff. Not that either of us would ever complain about that. She has no desire to be in a relationship after everything she's been through, and the store is her life. The shop was my grandma's before it belonged to my mom. It's the reason we came back to this town years after Mom fled it to escape her past.

When my grandma died, leaving my mom the shop and her house, I was surprised that she didn't even hesitate. She was practically packing up our stuff the next day. I may have only been a child, but I knew Mom had left Prairie Creek for a reason. I didn't fully understand it then, but I do now. *Boy, do I get it now.*

But the antique shop and a fully paid for house to raise me in was something Mom couldn't pass up. And even though things haven't always been easy for us here, I'm glad we made the move. Prairie Creek is my home. I have a life here, and friends that are as close as family.

Which brings me to the real reason I'm not feeling baseball today. *Emmy.*

I can't get her out of my head. Not since our kiss. She probably thinks it meant nothing to me, which is my fault since I freaked out when I saw Cal standing there.

This. Never. Happened.

Man, what a poor choice of words. There were so many other things I could have said. So many other things I should have said. But nope. I had to go and blurt out the worst possible thing imaginable. The minute those insanely stupid words came out of my mouth, I knew that they'd hurt her feelings. I could see it in the way her eyes widened. But mostly I could see it in the resigned set of her shoulders, in how swiftly she shut me out. Now she's ignoring me. Earlier, I passed her in the school hallway, and she quickly turned her head. Wouldn't even look at me. It's not how I wanted things to go down with us.

Kissing her was a mistake, yes, but not because I didn't want to. Hell, I've wanted to for longer than I care to admit. But Cal's like a brother to me. And Emmy is his *sister*. He's incredibly protective of her, and I know he won't like it if he finds out what happened between us.

Cal launches a pitch in my direction. It's a curveball low and outside. I go to block the ball like

I have done a hundred times, but it skips past me. I pop up quickly and scoop it off the ground.

"Dude, what's up with you today?" Cal asks, jogging over to me.

I blow out a breath, wishing I could tell him. Rarely do I keep anything from Cal. He knows everything about me. More than anyone else. It's not like we're chicks and share every single thought, but we always share the big stuff. And kissing Emmy sure as hell qualified as "big stuff."

"Nothin'," I say. My gaze flickers over to Josh out on the field and red hot anger sparks. It's only one fast glance, but Cal catches it. He's like that. Never misses a beat.

His eyebrows raise. "Is this about Saturday night?"

My heart stops. Did Emmy tell him? Hope emerges. If he knows and he's not pissed maybe this won't be a huge disaster. Hell, maybe there's a chance that Emmy and I can actually be together. I allow myself to picture it, and it's scary how much my heart wants it. I'm not a relationship guy. I like to date, but not commit. I've gotten an earful about it from many chicks over the years. There are lots of reasons for my aversion to commitment. Some of them have to do with my dad and all of the family drama I've dealt with. But mostly it's because baseball comes first. It always has. And girls don't always get that.

But Emmy does. She's lived in this world – my world – her whole life. And she's cool with it. More than cool with it. She likes it. Even though she doesn't play herself, she gets it. And I know she would play if she could. In fact, she tried when she was younger. Several years in a row she played rec softball. Honestly, she wasn't half-bad. But then she got pelted with the ball at the end of her last season, and that was the end of that. Every time the ball came near her after that she flinched. Couldn't get past it. I've seen that happen to guys before too. Luckily I've never been scared of the ball. I've been beaned more times than I can count, but when a ball comes at me I stand my ground. Hell, I challenge the chump to hit me. It's why I'm a good catcher. Cal has often joked that our bodies are made of steel. He's not scared of taking a hit either.

"I know Emmy and Josh got in a fight. Is that the real reason you took her home?" Cal pins me with a questioning look.

Looking down, I nod. Cold wind whisks over me. Pulling my catcher's mask further over my forehead, I glance up at the sky. The clouds are still threatening rain, but have yet to deliver.

"Why didn't you tell me that, man?"

I shrug. "She asked me not to."

"Since when do you take orders from my little sister?"

"I don't. I just figured it was none of my business, you know?"

"If that were true, you wouldn't have brought her home," he says, and I feel exposed. My excuses are pretty flimsy. I need to step up my game if I want to keep up this ruse. My stomach twists. *Man, I hate this.* "And anything having to do with Emmy is your business because it's my business. I thought we were in this together, man."

"She's not *my* sister." I bristle.

"Like hell she's not," he snaps. "You're part of our family, bro. You know that."

63

I do know that. Ever since Mom and I moved back to town the Fishers have been there for us. Even when this whole town treated my mom like a pariah, the Fishers defended her, invited her to dinners, and helped her fix up the house and shop. Mostly because Cal's mom, Maise, and my mom have been best friends since childhood. And, truthfully, I've always loved feeling like part of their family. If I can't get a handle on this thing with Emmy I'll risk losing that. All I've ever wanted was a family – a place to be accepted. There's no way I can let what I have with the Fishers go. *What the hell is wrong with me?* "Yeah, I know." Agitated, I rub the back of my neck with my free hand.

Emmy's lips.

Emmy's hands.

Emmy's face.

It's all I can think about, but I have to stop. If not, I'll ruin everything.

Cal eyes me funny. "What's going on, man? You've been keyed up ever since Saturday night. Did something happen between you and Emmy?"

"No," I burst out. His head cocks to the

side. *Dude, I need to calm down.* I yank off the catcher's mask and run a hand over my head. Air escapes through my lips. "I just don't think Emmy needs anymore brothers. She's made it pretty clear that one is enough for her."

Cal chuckles. "Yeah, that's probably true. And she has been carrying a pretty big chip on her shoulder lately. But she'll thank us for having her back one day, bro. You'll see."

I don't buy it, but I nod anyway as I place the catcher's mask back on.

"So you're back with the old ball and chain, huh?" Chase's voice carries on the breeze.

My head snaps up in his direction. He's talking with Josh.

"We were never broken up, bro," Josh says.

"That's not how it looked at the party," Chase says with a wink.

It feels like someone is sitting on my chest, and I fight to catch my breath.

"Screw you," Josh retorts, but a small smile plays on his lips. I know what that look is about, and it makes me want to shove my fist in his face.

65

I ball my hands at my sides. "She's back with that asshole?"

"News to me too, man," Cal shakes his head.

"Why? Why would she want to stay with him?" My heart pounds in my chest, red hot anger burning me up. Emmy's sad eyes and vulnerable expression fill my mind. She deserves someone so much better than him.

"You know how stubborn Emmy is," Cal reminds me, but I barely hear him past the blood rushing to my head.

"We've got to put a stop to this. It's gone on long enough."

"Whoa." Cal puts his arm up to steady me. "I don't want my sister dating that jerk either, but we can't do anything about it, man."

"Why not?" I step past Cal. "I can do somethin' about it right now."

"Okay." Cal's tone is wary. "I have no idea what's going on with you today."

I close my eyes, trying to steady my heart. "Sorry. I just hate that guy so much."

When I open my eyes, Cal's eyes are filled with understanding "Ah, I get it. This has to do with your mom."

Not at all. It has everything to do with the fact that I want to be with his sister, but I can't admit that. So I bob my head up and down.

"Look, man, you've gotta get past that. I know it's tough, but we have to play ball with that guy." Cal moves in closer. "But I'll tell you what. If he hurts my sister at all, I give you full permission to beat his ass."

I want to smile at that, but the thought of him hurting Emmy causes me to see red. Besides, if he hurts Emmy again, I won't need Cal's permission to unleash on him. And no one will be able to hold me back.

"Gladly," I say, spotting Josh across the field. When his head cranes in my direction, I narrow my eyes. He responds by tipping his head, a smug smile painted on his face. I don't break my gaze even though my insides are churning.

"I know I can always count on you." Cal grins.

I force a smile, but inside I feel sick. *Would he say that if he knew the truth?*

EMMY

Most people tell their best friend when they have their first kiss. Maybe their mom or their sibling. I told Christian. It's not like I sought him out to tell him. In fact, I hadn't planned to tell him at all. Honestly, I wasn't sure I wanted to tell anyone about my kiss with Miles. It wasn't the kind of kiss you want to relive. It was the kind of kiss you want to forget ever happened. And that was the plan.

Miles' mom gave us a ride home from the eighth grade dance. The minute she dropped me off I raced inside my house, hoping to outrun Miles' triumphant grin. I knew he was hoping for another kiss, but that wasn't happening. The house was quiet when I stepped inside, and I was a little surprised. I had assumed Mom would be waiting up, hoping for some juicy tidbit, some sliver of romance she could add into her latest novel. I wasn't sure if she really used our experiences as material for her books, but I imagined she did. Mostly because she was so desperate to talk to us about it. Most parents discouraged romantic endeavors, but my mom pushed us into them.

Grateful for the reprieve, I tip-toed toward my room, praying I wouldn't wake anyone. And that's when I saw him. Christian was sitting on the couch in the family room playing a video game. He had the sound on mute, so that's why I didn't hear it at first. Now I caught the faint clicking of the controller.

"Hey," he whispered over his shoulder as he continued playing.

"Hey," I answered softly. "Where is Cal?"

"In bed."

"Couldn't hang, huh?" I joked.

"Nope. He's a party pooper," Christian bantered back.

But we both knew the truth. Between school and baseball, Cal had been running himself ragged lately. Of course so had Christian.

"I'm surprised you're up." I walked into the family room so I could raise the volume of my voice a little.

"Nah, it's still early."

It wasn't that early, but for Christian it probably was. He'd always been somewhat of a night owl.

"So, how was the dance?" Christian paused the game and set down the controller.

It made me feel special that he'd stop the game for me. Silly, I know, but for some reason it felt significant.

"It was okay." After the words were out of my mouth, I knew they were a mistake. It was the first dance I'd attended. And I'd made such a big deal to the boys about going. The day before I went on and on about how I was older now. In fact, when Cal made jokes about Miles, I defended him, stating that I was mature enough to choose the right boy to go out with. I wasn't even sure I liked Miles. But he happened to be the only boy who asked me to the dance. Not that I would ever admit

71

that to my brother.

"Uh oh. That doesn't sound good."

"No, I didn't mean that. I meant it was a lot of fun." My lips wobbled a little when I smiled.

"How much fun?" Christian raised his eyebrows.

I rolled my eyes. "Now you sound like my brother."

Christian chuckled. "Okay, I'll back off."

"Thanks." *That was easy.* "I guess I'm glad I ran into you tonight instead of Cal. I thought for sure I was gonna get the third degree."

"Nah." Christian waved away my words and reached for the controller. My heart pinched a little. Clearly I'd bored him already. Light from the TV flickered over his face, painting his tanned skin in bluish hues. For a moment, I admired his chiseled features and strong jaw. I watched his fingers as they danced over the controller. Then I stared at his rock hard abs that clung to his tight t-shirt, and the muscles that protruded out of his upper arms. A lot of my friends were jealous that Christian spent so much time at my house. And I knew why. Christian was hot. I'd have to be an idiot not to notice that. Of course my friends also drooled all over my brother too, but I didn't get that at all. "I told Cal there was nothing to worry about."

His words hit me like a sucker punch. Why would he assume nothing would happen? Was I so repulsive that he thought no guy would ever make a move on me?

"For your information, Miles kissed me tonight." I stood up, puffing out my chest. "Yeah, that's right. I had my first kiss. And it was a damn good one," I put the emphasis on the word damn is if cussing would prove my maturity. "How's that for nothing to worry about?" I spun around on my heels, preparing to stalk out of the room in a dramatic fashion.

"Miles kissed you!" Christian spoke so loudly, I stiffened.

Whirling around, I shook my head desperately. "Shut up."

"Sorry." His eyes shifted back and forth.

"Cal will kill me if he finds out." I regretted my decision to tell Christian already.

"Fine, I won't tell him." Christian's eyes grew serious. "But tell Miles I'll be watching out for him. He better treat you right."

My heart flipped in my chest, my whole body warming. Smiling, I walked back to my room feeling light as air. It was like I was walking on puffy white clouds, my feet never hitting the floor. I'd like to say that I fell asleep dreaming of Miles and my first kiss. But it was Christian's words that I heard as I drifted off. And it was his face that filled my dreams.

****

I wake from a fitful night's sleep. Christian invaded my dreams last night too, and I blame him for all of my tossing and turning. I should be over the moon that Josh and I are still together. Yesterday he was so sweet. Possibly sweeter than he's ever been. He walked me to all of my classes, even held my backpack for me. And when I was cold at the end of the day he offered me his jacket. When he draped it over my shoulders I saw the jealous looks of the girls we passed in the halls. And I knew I should feel lucky, but instead I felt conflicted, torn, and kind of sick.

It's all Christian's fault.

Why did he have to go and kiss me like that, effectively stirring up all of my old feelings? Feelings I had worked really hard at burying. Feelings that never should have resurfaced. Especially not now.

Blowing out a frustrated breath, I toss off my covers and swing my legs off my bed. The pads of my bare feet hit the soft carpet, and I shuffle out of my room. Yawning, I step into the hallway and walk right into my brother's chest.

"Watch where you're going," he booms.

I wince, reaching up to touch my temple. "You don't have to yell."

"Mornin' to you too, Grump." He nudges me in the arm.

I stick out my tongue at him. Immature, I know, but I'm not feeling grown up today.

"You kiss Josh with that stinky mouth?" Cal curls his nose in disgust.

75

Clamping my mouth shut, I can't figure out which one is more embarrassing. My bad breath or Cal talking about me kissing Josh. And what made him say that anyway?

When I throw him a confused look, he nods. "Yeah, that's right. I know you two are still together."

"Yeah. So?" I cross my arms over my chest.

He shakes his head. "I just don't get why you still want to be with him. Neither does Chris."

"Christian knows?"

Cal nods. "We overheard Josh braggin' about it at practice. Chris was actually pretty upset."

My heart leaps. "He was? Why?"

"C'mon, it doesn't take a genius to figure out that Josh is not Chris's favorite guy in the world."

And with that explanation, my heart plummets. Christian's dislike of Josh has nothing to do with me. I should have known. "Move out of the way. I need to take a shower." Shoving Cal aside, I make my way toward the bathroom.

"Speaking of Chris," Cal says. "Go easy on

the guy."

I whirl around, perplexed. "What?"

"He thinks you're upset with him about Saturday night, but he was only trying to help."

When he was rescuing me from Josh or when he stuck his tongue down my throat? "Fine. Can I get ready now or do you have any more nagging to do?"

Cal whistles. "Dude, is it that time of the month or something?"

"Shut up." I swat at him.

"Can you two keep it down?" Mom stumbles out of her room, hair disheveled, her eyes heavy-lidded. She wears black pajama pants and one of Dad's t-shirts. It's about two sizes too big and swallows her whole. Mom is tiny. She's only five feet tall, and doesn't have an ounce of fat on her body. With Dad's giant shirt hanging off her and no makeup on her face, she appears childlike. "It's too early in the morning for your bickering."

Mom has never been a morning person. Before Cal and I drove, she could barely stay awake long enough to take us to school. And she never got dressed. Just hopped in the car in her PJ's, white-blond hair sticking up everywhere, indentations from the pillow painted on her cheek. Rarely do I see her in the morning now. In fact, sometimes when we get home from school she's still wearing her pajamas while she sits at her computer, writing furiously.

There's no way I would stay in my pajamas all day. Then again, I'm nothing like Mom. I enjoy order and schedules. Mom detests them. She lives in a state of chaos and is perfectly content with it. It makes my skin crawl. Even as a little girl I'd follow Mom around straightening and cleaning up. She used to tease me about it, but has since stopped. I like to think she sees the value in it now, but most likely she's tired of fighting me to be someone I'm not.

When I was younger, Mom tried and failed to bring out my creative side. She put me in art and creative writing classes. She attempted to teach me how to draw pictures and make up stories. But I would end up painting pages of symmetrical lines or writing out to-do lists. Finally, Mom gave up. I'm not sure she embraces who I am, but at least she gives me the freedom to be that person. However, she's made it clear that she doesn't understand me. That's okay, though, because I don't understand her either.

But I understand her well enough to know not to push her when she's tired. "Sorry," I mumble toward Mom while throwing Cal an exasperated expression. Then I slip inside the bathroom. After clicking the door closed, I groan. Keeping my feelings in check is going to be even more difficult than I anticipated. Every time Cal mentioned Christian this morning a million feelings kicked up inside of me like a pile of leaves on a windy day. I can still feel them spinning around, flapping against my ribs. I mistakenly thought that getting back together with Josh would make getting over Christian easier, but it seems to have the opposite effect. And I have the sinking suspicion it's only going to get worse rather than better.

CHRISTIAN

The bell on the door rings, the musty scent of the shop filling my senses as I step inside. Funny how certain smells can cause a flood of emotions and memories to surface. Other than my house and the Fishers' house, this place is where I spend most of my time. I practically grew up here among the trinkets and antique furniture.

Even before moving to Prairie Creek in fourth grade, our tiny apartment in Sacramento was filled with antiques. Every birthday and Christmas, a package would arrive from my grandma filled with treasures. Mom would carefully take them out of the box, and then consult her antiques magazine to see how valuable each piece was. She used to tell me stories about her childhood in Prairie Creek, about helping her mom run the shop. She and her mom were pretty close since her dad died when she was teenager. I could never figure out why she never wanted to visit her mom if they were so tight. But whenever I asked her about it, she got all sad and teary. So I stopped bringing it up.

"Hey." Mom's head pops up from behind the counter. Today she wears her thick, dark hair in a long braid down her back. When she steps around the counter, the bracelets that line her arm jangle. Her skirt is so long it hides her feet as she makes her way over to me. "How was your day?"

"Fine." I glance around. "Yours?" It's quiet, and I wonder if she had many customers.

"It was okay." Her smile appears forced.

Business has been slow lately. I spot a tattered paperback lying open on the counter. It's one of Maise's. "Slow day?"

She nods, shame written on her face. *Crap.* The last thing I want to do is make Mom feel bad. It's not her fault the shop isn't doing well. Antiques aren't exactly a booming business around here. Especially not in the winter. In the summer we get more tourists. Visitors are our bread and butter.

The regulars rarely come in here. I think they shopped here more often when Grandma owned it. Once Mom took it over, it seemed that no one in town would ever set foot in the place. But over the years, people have softened a little toward Mom. Occasionally, some of them pop in. Usually to buy a gift for someone.

"That's okay. Things'll get better," I say in the most reassuring voice I can muster.

Without meaning to I peer over my shoulder at the window overlooking the street. The glass is pristine, smooth. Not so much as a hairline fracture. But I remember when it was broken, shattered, vandalized. It was right after we moved here, and it was the first time I knew what real rage was. Watching my mom pick up the jagged pieces of glass into her hands while her shoulders shook and tears streamed down her face was too much for me. If I wasn't a puny little runt at the time, I might have taken matters into my own hands. I might have kicked some serious ass.

If it happens now, I definitely will.

No one messes with anyone I care about

now. They know better. I'm sort of known for my short fuse, but it doesn't bother me. Bothers the hell out of my mom though. She's always trying to soften me up, touting off the importance of having self-control. But I don't buy it. I've watched people walk all over my mom for too long. Mom is one of the calmest people I know, and it's done her no good. And if she's not going to stand up for herself, then she needs someone who will.

My mind flashes on the image of Josh fighting with Emmy at the bonfire party. What is it with girls letting men stomp all over their hearts? And why is the jerk always the guy they want?

"I hope so." Mom sighs, placing her hands on her hips. "If not, I'm gonna have to call him."

I know exactly who she's referring to, and there's no way in hell I'm letting her call him. "No," I say. "We'll figure it out on our own."

"And if we don't?"

"We will," I say firmly.

Her lips curl upward into an amused smile. "You're so stubborn. Always have been."

"It's part of my charm." I shrug.

She snorts. "It was part of his charm too."

"Don't." I hate when she does this. Compares the two of us. He's the last person I want to be compared to. He may be my biological father, but that's where our connection ends.

"Not saying it doesn't make it any less true, Chris."

She always has to get in one last statement. "And I'm the one who's stubborn? Ever think I might get it from you, not him?"

She chuckles. I like this side of her. In moments like this I can imagine what she must have been like when she was younger. Happy and carefree. Most of my life she's been stressed and exhausted, beaten down. "You may be right about that." She pats my cheek.

From my pocket, my cell vibrates. I yank it out and see a text from Cal about dinner tonight. Not meaning to, I frown.

Mom furrows her brows. "What?"

"Oh, nothing. It's just Cal." I wave away her concern.

"Is it about dinner? Maise called earlier to

invite me." Mom glances over at the row of antique clocks lining the wall. Most of them aren't set to the right time, but one of them is. "You can head on over now, and I'll meet you there in a bit."

"Actually." I scratch the back of my neck. "I think I might just eat at home."

"Why?" Her confusion is warranted. I've never turned down dinner at the Fishers. Mom works late most nights so dinner at our house is mac n' cheese, sandwiches, or frozen dinners.

"I've got a lot of homework. That's all." Turning around, I attempt to hide from her scrutinizing gaze.

"Chris, what's going on?" I should've known Mom wouldn't let up that easy. She scurries around me, blocking my path. "Are you and Cal in a fight or something?" She looks so panicky that guilt wraps around me, squeezing hard. The Fishers aren't *like* family to us. They *are* family. And, frankly, they're the only family we have. The look on Mom's face is a further reminder of how bad I messed up. And it's confirmation of the fact that I can't afford to do it again.

"No. Cal and I are cool. I promise."

I expect relief, but her face remains conflicted. "Then why won't you go over there?"

"I will," I blurt out.

There's that look of relief I was wanting. "Oh, good. You scared me for a minute." She touches my arm. "You can get your homework done after dinner."

"Yeah." I force my lips into a smile, steeling myself for the evening.

My phone vibrates again. Cal's wondering why I haven't responded. Blowing out a breath, I text back.

Me: Sorry. At the shop. On my way.

"All right." I hug Mom swiftly. "I'll meet you there."

"Okay." She smiles brightly.

Dread descends on me as I head out of the shop. Seating at the Fishers' dining table has always been the same. Cal and I sit next to each other with Mom and Emmy across from us, and Maise and Tim at each end. When we were kids, Emmy and I would kick each other from under the table sometimes when we were bored. Now I have no desire to kick her. I don't want to tease her or play the role of big brother. I want so much more from her than that. But I know it's wrong. I know I have to set aside my feelings. How am I going to endure an entire evening with Emmy sitting directly across from me? How am I going to look Maise and Tim in the eyes knowing that I made out with their daughter?

More importantly, how am I going to move past this?

How am I going to get over her?

****

I'm hoping to pull myself together before I get to the Fishers'. Too bad the drive doesn't give me enough time to do that. Prairie Creek is so small it only takes a few minutes to get anywhere. I pull up in front of their house and cut the engine. The street is quiet. When I glance at the house, I see Maise through the kitchen window. She's standing over the stove stirring something in a large chrome pot. The Fishers' house looks a lot like ours with the shuttered windows and wraparound porch. But even with the similarities, it's also a lot different too. Not so much in appearance. More in feel.

Our house is just that - a house. A place with walls, furniture and windows. A place to crash and stay sheltered from the elements. Cal's house is a home - full of laughter and noise.

Don't get me wrong. I like our house. And I like living with my mom. I'm definitely glad it's only the two of us. Over the years, she's dated a couple of guys. And let me tell you, I would not have been okay with her marrying one of those losers. No way would I have been a model son to some creepy stepdad.

And Mom's done her best to give me a good life. However, she works long hours and she's quiet by nature. Silence is the norm at my house. Not the case at all here. As if to prove my point, I hear loud chatter as I walk up to the front door. It's coming from an open window to my right. Maise and Tim are sharing the details of their day with each other. I shake my head at how funny their conversation is as Maise rattles on about something crazy one of her characters did. If I didn't know better, I might assume she was talking about a real person. And Tim's comments about his first grade students sound stranger than fiction.

Lifting my hand, I knock. When I hear footsteps from inside, I silently pray Emmy doesn't answer. I know I'll have to see her, but I'm not quite ready yet. Fortunately, it's Cal who answers the door. But the funny look on his face sends off warning signals in my head.

"Did you get my text, man?" Cal asks when I step inside.

"What text?"

"The one from a few seconds ago."

I shake my head. He must have sent it when I was driving.

"Chris." Tim materializes in front of me. "How ya doing?"

"Good." I nod.

"Glad to hear it." He pats me on the shoulder. "I'm looking forward to the start of the season. With the new line-up, you guys can't lose."

"Hey, Chris," Maise calls from the kitchen. "Tim, don't start in on him about baseball yet. He's barely stepped in the door."

"At least I'm talking about something that isn't fictional," he retorts, but his smile betrays that he's only joking with her.

"Oh, stop. You're lucky to be with a woman as interesting as me," Maise banters back. Tim saunters into the kitchen, grabbing Maise from behind and drawing her into his chest.

Cal shakes his head as if he finds the entire exchange disgusting. I start to chuckle, but it gets lodged in my throat. Emmy and Josh sit on the couch in the family room. I cough in an attempt to swallow down the anger that rises in my throat.

"What's *he* doing here?" I ask through gritted teeth.

Cal lowers his head. "That's what I was trying to tell you."

Ah, yes, the text. Now I wish I had gotten it. Then I might have gone home the way I initially wanted to. If I thought facing Emmy would be challenging tonight, watching her with this douchebag is going to be hell.

Her head is bent near his. He says something, and she giggles. When his hand lifts to touch her hair and she presses her cheek into his palm, my insides churn. *I cannot stomach this shit.* Her eyelids flutter, and I know what's going to happen. I've seen that look in her eyes before. I know I should turn away, but it's like when you pass a car accident on the freeway. You don't want to look because you're afraid you might see something gruesome. But then you have to look because you might see something gruesome. Seeing Emmy kiss this freak is pretty much the most gruesome thing I can imagine. And yet, I can't avert my eyes. As their heads get closer and their lips almost touch, something explodes inside of me. It's like my anger meter has reached its limit. Like I'm a pot boiling on the stove and now I'm spilling over.

I take a step forward, my hands shaking.

And I know this is it.

I'm going to wind up in jail for killing this jerk.

I can see it all playing out in my mind. Me

yanking him away from Emmy and pounding his smug little face in. And even as I think it, I know it's extreme. I mean, the guy's a dick, but he shouldn't be murdered for simply kissing his girlfriend. Except that she shouldn't be his girlfriend.

She should be mine.

Oh, hell.

Composing myself, I halt. What am I doing? I needed to stop these crazy thoughts.

Lucky for me, Tim enters the room. When he spots what's happening on the couch, he clears his throat loudly. That's one thing I've always liked about Cal's parents. They don't nag, and they're not harsh. They're gentle in their approach, but they're also clear. And it's clear to me that Tim doesn't want to see Josh kiss Emmy any more than I do.

Emmy comes out of her stupid Josh-induced fog, and snaps her head toward her dad. But before her gaze reaches him, it sweeps over me. She appears startled, but other than that I catch nothing. No conflict raging in her eyes. No sadness or anger. Clearly she's not wrestling with her feelings the same way I am. It shouldn't hurt, but it does. I should feel relief, but relief is that last thing I feel.

"The woman of the house has instructed me to find out what everyone wants to drink," Tim says. "But I should warn you that I tried waiting tables once in college, and I was fired after two shifts."

Cal chuckles. Emmy shakes her head and leaps up. Josh appears confused, and I feel a strange sense of satisfaction from this. He has no idea what's going on, but I do. Not only am I familiar with how Tim launches into one of his long, drawn-out stories, but this is one I've heard countless times before. But Josh hasn't. Frankly, I don't mind Tim's stories. And actually this one is pretty funny, albeit embarrassing. But apparently, Emmy wants no part in it.

"Dad, I'll help you get the drinks. I know what everyone wants," she says swiftly, grabbing her dad by the elbow and steering him out of the room.

"You seem to be everywhere that Emmy is,

Chris." Josh cocks one eyebrow at me.

For a split second I wonder if Emmy told him about our kiss, but then I shove the thought away. The guy has an ego the size of Texas. No way would he stay with Emmy if he found out she was making out with me last weekend.

"He's family." Cal's face hardens in a challenge.

Josh throws up his arms in surrender. "Relax. I was just making conversation."

"Maybe your conversational skills need some work," I respond dryly.

"I'm definitely not takin' lessons from you two." Josh's gaze shifts between Cal and I.

I open my mouth to respond when I spot my Mom's car pulling up to the curb outside. Cal's eyes widen. She deserves a warning about what she's walking into. "I'll be right back."

Cal nods. Josh glances out the window, spotting my mom. I'd give anything to get rid of this clown permanently. He's nothing but trouble. With my head down I hurry out of the family room. I'm just rounding the corner when I bump into

Emmy. Her scent washes over me, conjuring up memories of Saturday night. I step back from her abruptly.

"Um...sorry," she mumbles.

"For what? Bumping into me or inviting that asshole over?"

"Keep your voice down," she whispers. "That's my boyfriend you're talking about."

"Yeah, I know. And why is that?" I growl. "Why would you stay with him?" Before I can stop myself, I grab her arm.

"That's none of your business." She pulls away from me.

Footsteps sound on the walkway outside. My heart freezes. "I've gotta warn my mom about Josh."

Emmy's face softens. "I didn't know your mom was coming to dinner."

I shrug. It's not the admission I want. She doesn't get it. "I guess she'll have to get used to being around him."

She nods. Clearly she thinks I've resigned myself to the fact that she wants to be with Josh;

that she's chosen him. But that's not the case. Even if Emmy and I can't be together, I'll never be okay with her relationship with Josh.

"You know, since we play ball together," I add. Then I step around Emmy and open the door to greet my mom.

EMMY

I thought it would be easier if Josh were here.

It isn't.

If anything, it's worse. But when I found out Christian was on his way, I panicked. I wasn't sure how I'd face him all evening. Our kiss is all I can think about. It fills my head day and night, desire burning me up. I've tried everything to eradicate him from my mind, but nothing works. Not even kissing Josh. Every time I press my lips to his, its Christian's lips I imagine. Then I feel ashamed and dirty. Sometimes I wonder if Josh knows; if he can see right through me. But when I look into his eyes, I can tell he doesn't suspect a thing. Why should he?

I'm not exactly the cheating type. I'm the follower. The good girl. The one who goes with the flow. Besides, Josh thinks he's god's gift to women and that I worship the ground he walks on. Which I guess is my fault, since I have for most of our relationship. I've overlooked so many things I probably shouldn't have, and it would appear that I'm doing the same thing now. Only I know better. I'm only with him to protect my heart from the one person I truly want.

But whenever I'm in Christian's presence I want to abandon my plan. I want to dump Josh and throw myself into Christian's arms. However, that can never happen. Mainly because Christian doesn't want me that way. Not that it matters. Even if he did, it would never work out.

Christian is part of our family.

And our kiss is screwing things up. I can feel the tension between Christian and me like a tangible thing, and I worry that everyone can pick up on it. But no one else seems to notice. When I bump into Christian in the hallway before dinner, the anger on his face cuts to my heart. I think I see jealousy painted across his features. As hard as I try to fight it, hope arises, my heart skipping a beat.

But then he mentions his mom and I feel like crap. Of course this isn't about me. It's about Olivia. I should've known. Christian's dislike of Josh runs deeper than me. It runs deeper than all of us.

I never would've invited Josh tonight if I knew Olivia was coming. I try to explain this to Christian, but he's still angry. And I don't blame him. It's not uncommon for Olivia to come to dinner. Olivia and Christian eat here all of the time. Therefore, I should have asked. Perhaps I should have assumed, but I wasn't thinking. I was desperate, so I reacted. Not that I can say any of that aloud. I can't admit any of it.

My only option is to endure this night the best I can. As I trek into the family room to retrieve Josh, I find myself wishing I had magical powers that could make this entire night disappear. Then again, if I'm wishing for superpowers, maybe I should wish for something bigger. Like to go back in time and make my kiss with Christian disappear.

My heart squeezes at the thought, and I realize I don't want that. I should want that. God knows I should. But I don't. Even if it can never happen again, I don't regret it.

And that makes me feel even worse.

Guilt riddling me, I approach Josh. He and Cal are involved in some kind of pissing contest, and they both shut their mouths when they spot me.

I cross my arms over my chest, raising my brows. "Don't stop on my account."

"We were just talking baseball, baby." Josh opens his arm, motioning for me to step into it. Reluctantly, I do. Cal frowns.

"Sure you were," I mutter.

"What's that?" Josh asks.

"Nothing." I smile sweetly.

Cal shakes his head. "I'm gonna go find Chris and say hi to Olivia."

I feel Josh's stare boring a hole into the side of my face as Cal exits the room.

"You didn't tell me that *she* would be here," he says, his tone laced in betrayal.

Man, this night is a disaster. "I didn't know." I turn to him. "But Olivia is part of this family, so play nice." I don't usually speak to Josh like that, but there's no way I'm letting him disrespect Olivia. I love her like she's my own mom. In fact, there have been times when she was more of a mom to me than my own mother. Olivia is creative as well, but in a different way than my mom. And, since she runs her own business, she's more levelheaded, more organized. She gets me in a way my mom never has. I can't even count how many times Olivia has offered me a listening ear or a shoulder to cry on.

Besides, I don't even understand why he hates her so much. The scandal that blew up her life didn't hurt Josh. In fact, it's safe to say, it helped him.

Josh pulls away from me, his arm slipping from my shoulders. "When we started dating I had no idea how much family you had." He says the word "family" with sarcasm, and an edge of disgust.

"Would it have made a difference?"

"Probably."

Ah, always the romantic. "Thanks a lot." I scowl.

"What do you expect me to say?" He lowers his voice. "You know how I feel about Olivia."

Well, at least he's being honest. That's more than I can say for some people. Case in point, Christian appears in the doorway of the family room. His gaze sweeps over me, then lands on Josh. His lips curl downward.

"You can leave if you want," I whisper to Josh, a part of me hoping he will, while another part of me wants him to stay. Not so much because I want him here, but because it will be embarrassing if he ditches me in front of everyone again. Besides, I'm not sure my parents like him that much. If he skips out on dinner, they won't like him at all.

"*She* should leave. I've done nothing wrong."

I bite my lip to keep from saying what I'm thinking. It disgusts me how this town keeps making Olivia pay for something that happened so long ago. "She's my mom's best friend. She's not leaving," I say in a hushed voice, careful to make sure no one hears us. Anywhere else in town Josh could get away with talking bad about Olivia. But

102

not here. If anyone else hears what he's saying, they'll throw his ass out. And it makes me feel sick that I don't have the guts to do it.

"Fine." He throws up his hands. "I get it. I'll be on my best behavior." Leaning down, he kisses me swiftly on the mouth. "For you."

It's the kind of statement that used to make my heart soar. I used to live for moments like this. Now I see them for what they are. *Lines*. Words with no real meaning. Still, I force a smile, reminding myself that it's my fault he's here.

Not just in my house, but in my life.

"Thanks. C'mon." Grabbing Josh's hand, I guide him toward the dining room where everyone else has congregated. The scent of garlic and chicken wafts under my nose, causing my stomach to growl. I'm surprised by the reaction since my stomach is so nervous I doubt I'll be able to eat a bite. When Josh and I enter the dining room, everyone except for Mom is seated. She's still fluttering about like a butterfly, setting platters of food on the table. All eyes fall on us, and my chest tightens. No one speaks, and I find myself once again wishing to disappear.

But it's Olivia who breaks through the tense moment. She stands and steps toward me. "Emerson! It's so good to see you, sweetie." Olivia is the only person on earth that calls me by my full name. She's also the only person who calls my brother Callahan. But I don't mind. In fact, it would probably sound weird if she called me Emmy. Wrapping her arms around me, she pulls me into a tight embrace. "I feel like I haven't seen you in forever."

It's only been a couple of weeks, but I welcome the affection. Besides, I missed her too. The last few times she came to dinner I was out with Josh or Ashley.

Drawing back from me, her gaze lands on Josh. "You're Josh, right?"

Josh narrows his eyes and my insides coil. But then he nods. "Yep." It's not exactly a warm reception, but at least he doesn't say anything rude.

"Olivia." She sticks out her hand.

Josh looks at it, but doesn't take it. "I know who you are."

"All right." Mom claps her hands. "Dinner is on."

I'm grateful for the interruption. Throwing Olivia an apologetic glance, I yank Josh's arm, tugging him toward the extra chair Mom put out for him. As I slide into my chair, my eyes meet Christian's. He looks pissed. Like really pissed. Lowering my gaze, I take a deep breath. Mom sits at the head of the table and everyone starts passing the food around. Josh's arm brushes my elbow periodically as he scoops food onto his plate. Conversations spin around me, but I keep my head down willing the night to end.

Pretty soon my plate's filled with food, but I can't eat a bite of it. My stomach churns so hard, I've lost my appetite. My head bent, I push food around my plate with my fork. Apparently Josh's appetite is still intact though. Out of the corner of my eye, I see him shoveling in forkfuls as if he's never eaten before. Annoyance surfaces. He's ruined this night for me, and he's not fazed at all. *Typical.*

"Cal, did you see that play that Aaron made

at practice yesterday?" Christian says.

"Yeah, dude, that was awesome."

"I know. He's the best shortstop we've had. It's gonna suck for you guys when he's gone next year, Josh," Christian says, an edge to his voice.

My head snaps up. Josh's face reddens.

"I'll be on shortstop then, so we'll be fine." Josh seethes.

"If you really want them to put you on shortstop you better step up your game." Christian lets out a tiny chuckle.

"Yeah, man, you've bombed at second the last couple of practices," Cal interjects.

Seriously. Get me the hell out of here.

"I have not." Josh bristles.

"Boys," Mom interjects. "No more sports talk about the table."

"Okay. Why don't you tell us how Bracken is? Didn't you say he was going in for chemo today?" Cal laughs, humoring her.

"Why, yes, actually. So, you do listen to me." Mom beams.

Josh appears puzzled.

I shake my head. "Bracken is one of Mom's newest characters," I explain, desperately wishing I was one of Mom's characters, too so I could hide inside the pages of a book.

Josh leans down to whisper in my ear as Mom launches into her latest plot. "Don't take this the wrong way, but your family is weird."

Trust me, I'm aware.

Josh's lips graze my cheek when he pulls back. Pausing, he stamps a kiss on my skin. But it doesn't feel like an act of love, more like he's marking his territory. Glancing up, I catch Christian staring at us, his eyes steely. He looks ready to pop a fuse. It almost seems like he's jealous, but I know better. This whole dinner I feel like I'm in the middle of a war between these boys. The funny thing is that I'm not sure it has to do with me at all. I'm nothing more than the tennis ball being volleyed back and forth. The object they are using to inflict harm in their stupid battle. And it's giving me a massive headache.

Tired of it, I excuse myself and hurry to the restroom. Once inside, I close the door firmly and

107

blow out a breath. My nerves are frayed, my insides quivering. It's my fault. I set this whole thing in motion. Now I want nothing more than to quit the game. To blow the whistle, signaling the end.

Fortunately, dinner is almost over. Josh had mentioned earlier that he had homework to do later, so I'm praying he'll take off pretty quickly. Then I can finally get my wish. I can escape into my room and hide under the covers.

Gathering courage, I take three deep breaths. One. Two. Three. Then I reach for the door knob and turn it. With my head held high, I step into the hallway. The minute I do, Christian comes around the corner.

Super. Just my luck.

I try to skirt around him, but he sidesteps, blocking my path.

"Why him?" he growls.

I freeze. "What?"

His face is so close to mine I can feel the warmth of his breath. My pulse spikes. "Why him?" He repeats. "Out of all the guys in the world, why do you have to date him?"

I step back, my heart hammering. His proximity is making my head spin. I'm grateful when my back hits the wall, knowing it will keep me upright. "He asked."

"That's all it takes, huh? You'll just say yes to anyone who asks?"

When he puts it like that, it sounds pathetic. "I don't know." I don't know anything when Christian's standing this close to me.

He grunts, running a hand over his head. "I mean, you had to know it was going to be awkward bringing him around my mom and me."

"My dating Josh has nothing to do with you. It's not like I consider you in every damn decision I make."

"Clearly." His eyes flash.

I sigh. Man, I hate fighting with Christian. "I didn't mean it like that." Truth is, when I met Josh I didn't make the connection between he and Christian. And once I figured it out, it was too late. We were already dating.

"Oh, I think it's exactly how you meant it." He pushes past me, his shoulder bumping mine.

After he vanishes into the bathroom, slamming the door, I lean my head against the wall. I've screwed up royally, and I'm not sure how to fix it.

I'm starting to wonder if it can be fixed at all.

CHRISTIAN

I'm not a morning person. I'm a night owl. I walk around like a zombie for most of the day, only to get a second wind around nine o'clock at night. In fact, I threatened to quit playing baseball the first time we had a game at eight am. My mom, on the other hand, is up every morning at the buttcrack, so she's never understood my aversion to mornings.

After last night, I wanted nothing more than to stay in bed all day. Truth is, I'm scared of seeing Josh at baseball practice this afternoon. Not because I think the wuss can hurt me. No, it's because I'm scared I won't be able to keep my emotions in check around him. All night I dreamt of beating him to a bloody pulp, and I'm a little worried I might try to turn that into a reality once we get out on that field.

The scent of freshly brewed coffee fills my senses as I head down the hallway. I've already showered and dressed, and a chill runs through me as I enter the kitchen. As if on cue, the heater kicks on. Mom sits at the kitchen table sipping coffee and picking at an English muffin. She's dressed in a long skirt and floral top, her hair is in a loose bun, and her face is bright.

"Good morning," she trills.

"Yeah," I mumble, reaching for the coffee pot. I'd pour it straight into my mouth if Mom would let me. But I'd tried that before, and it didn't go over well. So instead, I grab a mug and fill it to the brim. The coffee is so hot it burns my tongue, but I don't care. If I'm going to have to face Emmy with Josh today, I'm going to need a lot of this stuff.

"Why don't I hook you up to a coffee IV?" Mom teases.

"Is that a thing?" I banter back. "Because if so, sign me up."

"You wish." After one last bite of her

muffin, Mom stands, wiping her palms on a napkin. She drops her plate into the sink, and turns to me. "Okay, I'm off to the shop. Have a good day at school and practice."

"Hey," I stop her before she can walk away. "Are you okay?"

"Yeah." She knits her eyebrows together. "Why wouldn't I be?"

"I know that it must have been hard having dinner with Josh last night."

"He was fine," she says evenly. That's Mom. She doesn't get rattled easy. "Besides, I get it. I know why he doesn't like me. He's protective of his family. I can respect that."

"But why? It doesn't make sense. What happened was before he was even born. You're not hurting his family now."

"I'm sure his mother has poisoned him against me since he was a little boy," Mom says.

"But why?"

She shakes her head. "Let's just say that Heather and I were very good friends once upon a time. After everything blew up, she harbored a lot of resentment toward me."

"I still don't get it."

Stepping toward me, she pats my cheek. "Josh is hotheaded, Christian." She shrugs. "And I know someone else who is just like that."

I stiffen, hating that she's comparing me to him. We are nothing alike. "What happened was so long ago. Don't you ever get tired of people acting like it was yesterday? I mean, shit, whatever happened to forgive and forget?"

"Language," Mom warns. She's the only parent I know who doesn't allow her teenage son to say a cuss word every now and then.

But I know better, so I mutter, "Sorry."

Satisfied with my apology, Mom says, "This town doesn't forgive and forget very easily. People around here have gotten good at holding grudges."

I shake my head. "It's stupid."

"Yes, it is." She smiles. "But I can't change it. I can't control what others think about me. I can only control what I think about me, and I'm content with who I am. I know I've made mistakes in life. Including one really huge mistake. But I've

114

learned from it, and I'm a better person now."

"If only everyone else could see that."

"It's okay if they don't. Their opinions don't matter to me." Leaning over, she gives me a swift hug. "The only opinions that matter to me are mine, yours, and that of my closest friends."

Mom has always seen the world through rose-colored glasses. Sometimes I wish we could trade. Just once I'd like to see through her lenses. But I don't see what she does. To me the world is a much darker place.

"Now I really have to get going." She glances down at my coffee cup. "Go easy on that stuff. I don't need you having a heart attack at seventeen."

"Eighteen," I correct her.

"Not until next month." She waggles her fingers at me. "You're already growing up fast enough. Don't rush it."

I grin at her as she snatches up her purse and hurries toward the front door. After she leaves, I suck down the remaining coffee in my mug and then yank my lunch out of the fridge. When I spin around, I spot Cal pulling up in front of my house. Since Mom and I share a car, Cal drives me to school most days. But it doesn't bother me. It makes sense for Cal and me to carpool. We're always together anyway.

I race into my room to grab my backpack off the floor. Then I walk down the hallway and out the front door. It's not until after I lock it that I notice her. She's sitting in the passenger seat next to Cal. I inhale sharply. It's not like Emmy never rides with us. Before she got her license she rode with us all the time. Even since she got her own car she sometimes chooses to tag along with her brother. Then again, she's always been like that.

When we were kids it used to drive me nuts. How she would follow us around like she was Cal's shadow. She seemed to be everywhere. We could never shake her. And she was annoying, always whining or needing help. I could never understand why Cal put up with her. In fact, he not only put up with her, but he encouraged her to hang out with us. It didn't make sense.

Until the day I witnessed something that

made it all clear.

It was a hot summer afternoon. Cal and I had spent all morning riding bikes around the neighborhood. It was the one day we had to ourselves because Emmy had popped the back tire of her bike earlier that morning. She had to wait for her dad to come home that evening before it could get fixed. Cal attempted to talk me into doing something different so Emmy could take part, but I insisted on riding bikes. Cal gave in, mostly because I had gotten a brand new bike a few days before. And he knew how much I loved riding it.

I had to take a break to go to the bathroom, but Cal stayed outside. When I headed in the house, I heard Emmy and her mom talking. They couldn't see me because they were in Maise's office, and I had come in through the garage door in the kitchen. But their voices were loud, so I could hear every word.

"Please, Mom, I'm bored," Emmy whined, and I cringed. I heard that whiny voice in my nightmares. Holding my breath, I prayed she wouldn't figure out I was inside the house. The last

117

thing I wanted was for her to beg me to play with her. I'd finally gotten a break.

"Well, then, find something to do," Maise instructed her.

"There's nothing to do," Emmy responded in that same whiny tone. "Cal is riding his bike so there's no one to play with."

"You're a big girl. You can figure it out."

"Can't you take a break from your writing and play a game with me or something?"

I thought about all the games my mom and I played at home. We had a whole closet full of board games. But it was card games that Mom liked best. And I remembered her telling me that she and Maise used to play cards all the time when they were younger. I was sure Maise would take her up on the offer and then I'd be home free.

"Why can't you use your imagination? Why do you always have to have someone to entertain you? When I was a little girl I didn't need anyone to play with me. I made up worlds in my head. I could keep myself company. Why can't you be like that?" There was disappointment in Maise's voice, and it turned my stomach. My mom never talked to me like that. She always told me how special I was. How I was unique and amazing. "I swear, sometimes I wonder if you're really my child. You're nothing like me at all."

"No, I'm not!" Emmy shot back. "And I hope I never am!"

"Don't you dare talk to me like that, young lady." I'd never heard Maise so angry. I cowered in the kitchen.

"When I'm a mom I'll spend time with my daughter!" Emmy kept going. She had balls, I'd give her that.

"Not if she's anything like you, you won't, trust me."

I winced at her words. A frustrated sob tore down the hallway, reaching my ears. Loud footsteps told me that Emmy was running back to her room.

"Emmy," Maise called after her. "I didn't mean it."

A door slammed, and I flinched. Pressing my back to the wall, I waited for Maise to go after Emmy. But instead, the door to Maise's office clicked closed. Then I heard the sound of typing on a keyboard. Was she really not going to make up with Emmy? Was she not going to take away the hurtful words? I couldn't imagine my mom doing that. Rarely did she say something out of anger toward me, but when she did, she apologized immediately. Taking a deep breath, I pushed off the wall and trekked down the hallway.

I was dangerously close to peeing my pants now and I barely made it to the bathroom before I started going. Luckily it all got in the toilet. When I headed back into the hallway, Emmy's sobs slipped under her doorframe. I wanted to ignore them. I wanted to get back outside to riding my bike, to hanging out with Cal. What I wanted more than anything was to go back to enjoying my Emmy-free day, but I couldn't do that.

The little boy who always wished for a relationship with his own dad couldn't get the sound of Emmy's cries out of his head. I knew what it felt like to be rejected by a parent. And, let me tell you, nothing sucked worse. Now I understood why Cal never pushed Emmy away, and why Emmy clung to him like he was her lifeline. Apparently he was.

Taking a few tentative steps forward, I rapped twice on Emmy's door. When she didn't immediately answer, I rapped two more times, and then a third and fourth quickly. It was Cal's secret knock. The door swung open. Emmy stood before me, tears streaking her face, her pigtails loose and messy. She didn't say a word. Just sniffed, and wiped a hand under her nose.

"Wanna come outside with me? I'll let you try out my new bike."

"Really?" Her eyes widened. Already some of the sadness was leaving her eyes, the usual brightness returning.

I nodded.

She bit her lip, hesitating a moment. "But what if I break the tire like I did on mine?"

"You didn't break it. You popped it," I corrected.

When her eyes darkened, I regretted my words.

"But it doesn't matter. Even if you break it,

I won't be mad. It's just a thing. It's not like it's a person."

A broad smile broke out on her face. "Okay. Thanks."

The truth was that I didn't want her to break my bike. It was the nicest thing I'd ever owned. And luckily she didn't screw it up at all. But even if she had, I'd like to think I wouldn't have regretted my decision. I may have only been a child, but there was wisdom in my words. The bike was only a thing. Emmy's a person, and she's more important than any material object ever will be.

"Hey," Emmy says now, stepping out of the car when I approach.

I'm taken aback by the greeting. I wasn't expecting her to get out of the car to say hi, "Hey," I speak warily. "Where's your car?"

"In the shop," she explains.

"Tell him why." Cal raises an eyebrow in her direction.

She wears a challenging look. "It needed maintenance."

"Yeah. After being driven into a pole," Cal

122

interjects.

"A pole?" My insides tighten. "Are you okay?"

She holds her arms out. "As you can see, I'm fine."

She's fine all right. Her tight jeans and sweater hug her in all the right places, showing off every supple curve. Clearing my throat, I force my head away from her sexy figure. Not that it helps much. When I look up, my gaze locks in on her long silky hair, shimmering eyes, and plump kissable lips.

"The pole didn't fare as well though," Cal jokes.

"It's no big deal," she says in an exasperated voice. "I just grazed it with my fender when I was trying to park at the mall."

"Yeah. At the mall," Cal says. "And then after she crashed into the pole she still went in to shop."

"It was the last day of the sale, and I really wanted this top." She glances down, and my gaze follows. *I gotta say it was not a bad choice.*

"We really gotta work on those priorities," Cal says. As I continue staring at her top, I firmly disagree with him.

"When did this happen?" I'd never seen the top before. Trust me, I would have noticed it.

"Yesterday afternoon," she answers.

"You didn't say anything at dinner last night," I point out.

"Would you? Probably didn't want everyone to find out what a terrible driver she is." Cal's lips twitch at the corners.

"I'm so getting a ride with Ashley tomorrow," Emmy says with a groan.

"Just don't drive by the mall." Cal guffaws.

Emmy shakes her head. Then she reaches down to grab her backpack off the floor. "Anyway, Christian, you can have the front."

"No, that's okay."

"C'mon, we both know the back is too cramped for you." She smiles. "I insist."

"Well, if you insist then there's no reason to fight it."

"Right?" Cal chuckles. "Miss Stubborn over

here never changes her mind."

I laugh too. It feels good to be bantering with the two of them. It almost makes me forget about everything that's transpired over the past week.

Emmy sticks out her tongue at us.

"Very mature," Cal teases her.

"I learn from the best." She opens the back door and slides into the car.

After sitting down in the passenger seat, my gaze finds Emmy's in the rearview mirror. When our eyes meet, she grins, giving me a subtle nod. And then I know why she gave me the front seat. She's calling a truce. I'll gladly take it.

EMMY

At first I wasn't sure it was a good idea to ride with Cal this morning, but now I'm glad I did. I hated how things felt between Christian and me last night. It was weird and awkward, so unlike the way we are around each other. Being around Christian is usually as easy as breathing. I've known Christian most of my life. It's hard to imagine my life before he was in it. I mean, I know there was a time when he wasn't. I have vague memories from before he and his mom moved to Prairie Creek.

Most of them involved that annoying neighbor kid that Cal used to hang out with. Keith, I think his name was. He's since moved, thank goodness. He liked giving me wedgies and pulling my hair. When I would complain about him Mom would shake her head and say that's how boys show you they like you. I decided then and there that I never wanted a boy to like me.

My stance on that has since changed.

Although, sometimes it still feels that way. *Love hurts*. That's what I keep learning, and I don't like it one bit. Also, I don't think it's supposed to.

However, it seems to be the case when it comes to me. I'm always wanting the affection of someone who doesn't want me back. It's like the curse of being Emmy or something. Except for Cal. He's the one person on this planet who I don't have to perform for. He loves me no matter what. I used to think of Christian the same way, but things feel different now.

But I don't want to fight with him. If I can't have him the way I want to, then I want to go back to how things were. Back to when he was being all big-brotherly and protective. Back to when we joked and bantered like siblings. And this morning we've found that old rhythm. Cal turns on the radio and the boys sing along to some Bruno Mars song, crooning at the top of their lungs. It sounds like

127

two dogs dying, but it makes me laugh so hard my stomach hurts.

It's perfect. The best morning I've had in a long time.

As Cal pulls into the school parking lot, Christian belts out the last line in the song. I throw my head back, a stream of laughter spilling from my lips. Christian's eyes catch mine in the rearview mirror, and he laughs too. I love this. This connection with Christian, where we can communicate without saying a word. It's been like this since we were kids. One raised eyebrow or curve of our lips from across the room could convey so much. We perfected the art of speaking without words over the years, sitting across from each other at the dinner table. Even Cal has teased us about it. The two of them may be best friends, but there's no denying our connection.

However, reality punches me in the gut when I see Josh standing a few feet away watching us. Christian's face grows serious. I close my mouth, my laughter ceasing. The car quiets, tension returning.

128

Cal guides the car into a parking space, oblivious to what's happening.

As I gather up my belongings, Cal and Christian exit the car. By the time I step outside, Christian is already across the lot. His back is to me, his shoulders rigid. He doesn't even look back. Not even when Cal jogs toward him.

The moment is broken.

Or perhaps it was never there to begin with.

****

The cafeteria is already packed by the time Josh and I get there. Usually I walk to lunch with Ashley since she and I have the class before this together. But when we stepped out of math, Josh was waiting for me, leaning against the wall, one leg bent like he thought he was posing for an ad in a catalogue. And he did look good. So why didn't I feel anything? In the past, Josh always had the capacity to make my heart skip a beat. One look, one smile, one touch is all it took to get my pulse racing. Now it's like I've flat-lined. And it's happening at the worst time.

Josh is finally giving me the attention I've always longed for. Ashley can't stop gushing about it. If only I could drum up the same excitement. Then again, Ashley's always been pretty giddy about my relationship with Josh. She's actually the one who introduced us. She was dating Chase at the time, and she was anxious for me to date a guy on the team so we could double.

When my gaze sweeps the room, I find Ashley sitting with the baseball team. It's where we normally sit, and I know it's where Josh is headed. It causes my stomach to tighten. As we near the table, I look over at Cal and Christian.

Before Ashley and I became friends I never sat with the baseball team. Not because I couldn't. I knew Cal would be cool with it, but I never wanted to use my brother as a way to make friends. Besides, I felt like I should have a life separate from him. So I used to sit out in the quad with my former friends. I guess you can call them the nerds. Ashley does. But even though none of them like me anymore, I can't call them that. It feels like a betrayal. Especially because deep down I know I belong more with them than I do here.

Often I feel like an imposter.

When Ashley spots me she leaps up. "Hey, girl." Her blond hair swishes around her shoulders, the scent of her expensive perfume wafts through the air. She definitely belongs here. It was she who first dragged me to this table. I had hemmed and hawed, explaining that this was my brother's turf, but she insisted I was being ridiculous. Her boyfriend at the time was at this table, and that made it as much ours as my brother's, she said. So I followed just like always.

It's what I'd gotten good at -following.

Ashley links her arm through mine and ushers me toward the table while whispering in my ear, "Oh, my gosh. Wasn't that so romantic how Josh was waiting for you after class? I really think he feels bad about the other night. He's like a changed man."

She's right. He is, and I can't figure out why. Ashley may believe he has pure intentions, but I know better. Something's up.

Ashley must sense my hesitation because

she squeezes my arm tighter. "Don't you think it's romantic, Emmy?"

"Yeah." I nod, and force a smile.

After we sit down, I notice Josh has already found a seat across the table with Chase and Nolan. I hate that I feel relief about it. He's been practically attached to my hip all week, and I need some breathing room. It's odd, because last week I wanted nothing more than for Josh to notice me, to put some effort into our relationship. Now that he has I want him to leave me alone. *Why is that?*

The minute my gaze floats to the other side of the table, I know exactly why it is. Christian's head bobs up, his neck craning in my direction. Cheeks warming, I glance down at my hands. I seriously need to get a grip.

"Emmy, are you even listening to me?" Ashley's voice cuts into my thoughts.

"Um…I'm sorry. What were you saying?" I return my focus to my best friend, attempting to abandon all thoughts of Christian. Of course that's easier said than done. As hard as I try to listen to Ashley's words, my mind keeps replaying my kiss

132

with Christian. It's the only thing I can think about lately. It consumes my thoughts day and night, and I wish it would stop. But when I hear the words "party" and "Friday night" I perk up.

"A baseball party?"

"Yeah. Aren't you going?"

I bite my lip, my eyes flickering over to Josh. "I don't know."

"Oh, come on, you know he's going to invite you." She smiles. "And you're going to invite me. Also, I know just the outfit you can borrow of mine." Ashley's always trying to dress me like I'm her own personal paper doll. Which is fine since she has a great sense of style. Not that mine is bad. I dress pretty cute most days. A lot cuter than I used to dress. Then again, everything I know about fashion I learned from Ashley.

"That sounds fun, but I'll have to let you know."

Ashley rolls her eyes and blows out a frustrated breath. Turning her head, she says, "Josh, you're gonna invite Emmy to go with you to the party on Friday night, right?" My chest tightens. I'd never talk to Josh like that. Of course, if I did he'd probably embarrass me in front of the entire table. Ashley's like that though. She's pushy. Everyone knows it. That's probably why she gets away with it. It's also probably why she can't keep a boyfriend.

"Of course." Josh grins in my direction. "I was going to ask her later today, actually."

"Sorry. Beat you to it." Ashley throws him a wink before returning her attention to me. "See. Sometimes a girl's gotta take action. It wouldn't kill you to be a little more assertive."

"I tried that last Friday night, remember? A lot of good it did me."

"It did you a lot of good," Ashley points out. "Josh has never been so into you."

Is that the real reason Josh is acting like this? Is it because I finally stood up for myself? I assumed he liked when I was submissive, but maybe he doesn't want a girlfriend who does everything he says. Maybe he has more depth than I thought. Hearing laughter, I glance over. Josh and his friends are throwing spitballs toward the band table.

So, clearly not. Clearly that was wishful thinking.

At the other end of the table Cal and Christian are hunched over in conversation, no doubt strategizing for their first scrimmage next week. I recognize the intense expression and strong set of Christian's mouth. And I find myself wanting nothing more than to get up, walk over there and plant myself next to Christian. I want to take his face in my hands and kiss him the way he kissed me last weekend. I want to confess my feelings to him.

But I know that would be stupid on so many levels. So I stay planted in my seat, listening to Ashley drone on about the party on Friday night and faking smiles of adoration in my boyfriend's direction.

CHRISTIAN

Prairie Creek is full of open fields. As a kid I loved to ride my bike over the dirt mounds and race through the vast expanses of land. When I got a little older, Cal and I would go four-wheeling out in the country. Now the fields provide the perfect venue for parties. Out in the middle of nowhere we aren't bothering anyone. The police don't get called, parents don't get mad about their house getting trashed. It's a win-win.

Tonight's party takes place on the outskirts of town at Old Willis's Farm. Years ago, an old man named Fred Willis lived here. Legend has it that he tried to kill his wife when he found out she was cheating on him. After she ran off, he went bat-shit crazy and the whole town was afraid of him. When he died, the property was willed to his son who lives in New York. But by that time the house was a dump and he didn't want it. Now it sits empty, rotting away. Most of the kids in town are still scared to go anywhere near this property. Some adults too. That's why it's the perfect location for a party. Lots of open space and an available barn if we need to take shelter.

Already there is a bonfire burning and a couple of kegs set up. Kids are everywhere, laughing, chatting, and making out. I weave through the crowd searching for Cal. We showed up together, but I lost him almost immediately when I started up a conversation with Palmer. It's weird because we were talking about the scrimmage next week and normally Cal's all about baseball. But he's been acting off all night.

When I find Cal he's lip-locked with some strange brunette. I wonder if this is the mysterious Melissa he's always raving about. I've yet to meet his college girlfriend, and sometimes I tease him that she must be fictional. He doesn't like that very much. Once Cal and the mystery girl come up for air, I instantly recognize her. *Nope. Not Melissa.*

"Hey, you know Gabby, right?" Cal points to the brunette.

"Yeah, I think we had science together last year."

She nods. "I think so." Her voice is odd, all high-pitched and squeaky. Even worse than Ashley's, and that's saying something.

When Gabby goes to get a drink, I yank Cal aside. "What about Melissa?"

"What about her?" Cal is already slurring his words. I notice two red Solo cups on the ground near where he was sitting with Gabby. That's not a good sign. He must be slamming them down. Guess I'm driving us home. Usually Cal's the responsible one.

"Well, what if she finds out you're at some party making out with another girl?" He may be drunk, but I need him to see reason. Even though I've never met Melissa, I know he's really into her.

"She won't give a rat's ass." He waves away my words with a shaky hand. "In fact, she's probably at some college party doing some frat boy."

Understanding washes over me. "So you guys broke up?'

Frowning, he nods.

"I'm sorry, man."

Cal shakes his head. "I'm not. I'm glad. Now I can be with whoever I want whenever I want. I don't have to be tied down to one girl. This stallion," He points to himself, "needs to roam free."

"Okay." I place a hand on his arm. "Let's reign it in their, horse boy." Rarely do I see "Drunk Cal" and it's pretty entertaining. But he's still my best friend, and I've always got his back. Tonight, having is back means making sure he doesn't make a fool of himself.

Gabby returns and Cal's all over her again. *Oh well.* That'll probably keep him out of trouble. Or at least keep him entertained. And, really, it's the best way to get his mind off of Melissa.

"Hey, Christian," a flirty female voice interrupts my thoughts.

I turn around, coming face-to-face with a

pretty dark-haired girl. It takes a minute for me to remember that we've met before.

"Selena, right?"

She smiles. "You remembered?"

"Of course." Glancing back at Cal, I realize that he has the right idea. If Gabby can help him get over Melissa, then maybe Selena can help me get over Emmy. "You alone?" I ask her.

Her grin deepens. "Yeah. You?"

"Yep." A cool breeze whisks over my skin.

"I guess it's my lucky day." She shivers, and I place an arm around her shoulders.

"I guess it is." I guide her forward. "Can I get you a drink?"

"Sure." She nestles in closer as we head toward the kegs.

Hayes is standing near the kegs passing out red Solo cups. He helps me pour beer into two of them. I don't know Hayes that well. He's a year younger than Cal and me, but he's a damn good hitter. Left handed too. He got pulled up to varsity last year when he was only a sophomore. At first I wasn't sure about him. Mostly because he was always making jokes and being goofy. But the first time I saw him hit the ball, all of my doubts vanished. He's the real deal.

"Have fun, man." He winks at me as Selena and I turn away from the keg, both of us fisting our filled cups. The bitter scent of beer fills my senses.

"I will," I assure him.

Lowering her head, Selena blushes. She really is pretty with her dark skin and long silky hair. Not only that, but she's got a great body.

"So, you ready for your first scrimmage this week?" She asks, surprising me.

"You know our schedule?"

She shrugs, daintily sipping her beer. Foam coats her lips and she licks it off slowly. She's no novice. My insides flip. "Our whole team does."

"Oh, that's right. You play softball."

"Second year on varsity." She smiles proudly.

Pretty and a softball player. *Where has she been all my life?* She saunters toward a large tree looming overhead and leans her back against it. I prop one of my hands against the rough bark and am about to take a swallow of my beer when I remember how inebriated Cal is. Lowering the beer, I sigh. I could've really used it to take the edge off. After I set it on the ground I glance at Selena, and she bats her eyelashes at me. Then again, maybe I don't need alcohol tonight.

When her eyes meet mine, she smiles, and I know it's an invitation. I don't think I even needed one. The chick's been sending me signals from the minute we started talking. However, I can't shut off the manners my mom's taught me over the years. Lowering my head, I angle my face toward hers. She holds her beer near her waist and raises her chin. Our lips almost touch when I see Emmy. She's walking in my direction holding Josh's hand. Ashley saunters beside her, her gaze bouncing around as if she's looking for someone. Which I'm sure she is. Probably looking for her latest victim. Josh peers over at Emmy and says something that makes her giggle. And it's all I can take. Closing my eyes, I press my lips to Selena's.

As she kisses me back, I do my best to lose myself in her so I can forget about the one girl I can't stop thinking about. The one girl I can't have.

The only girl I really want.

EMMY

The last thing I want to see when I show up to the party is Christian making out with some other girl. But that is literally the first thing I see. And not only is he kissing her, but he has her pinned up against a tree as if he wants to do much more than that. My gaze jumps to his hands in her hair, his fingers tangling in the strands, and my stomach sours. The bill of his baseball cap is pressing into her forehead, and I wonder if it hurts. Not the kiss. The bill of the cap on her forehead. I don't have to guess what the kiss feels like. I know exactly what it's like to kiss Christian, to have his fingers in my hair, to feel his palm against my cheek.

Man, why am I thinking about this at all?

"Helloooo, Emmy." Ashley waves her hand

in front of my face.

"Oh, sorry." I blink as if coming out of a daze.

"What's going on with you?" Ashley's eyebrows knit together. "Josh was asking if you wanted a drink and you were just totally spacing out."

Josh stares at me wearing a pensive look. Then he peers over in Christian's direction (who is still kissing that random girl) before returning his attention back to me. My insides churn.

"Sorry. Sometimes I just zone out. You know me." I force a giggle, and Ashley joins in. I'm not stupid, but every once in awhile it behooves me to play the dumb blond. Besides, Ashley likes it. She hates when I get all "brainy" as she calls it. Really she's referring to me being rational or mature, but whatever. "No, I'm not drinking, remember? I drove. Go ahead and get one for yourselves though."

"You sure?" Ashley asks, but Josh is already making a beeline for the keg.

"Yeah." I'm surprised she's even pushing
145

this. I never drink. It's one of the main reasons I always offer to drive. Well, that and the fact that I like knowing I can leave when I want. Thank god Dad's mechanic was able to fix my car fast. If I hadn't gotten it back today I might not have even come to this party. Ashley never lets me drive her car, but she also never refrains from drinking, so having her as designated driver is pointless.

"Cool. Thanks," she says.

When she heads over to the keg, I spot Josh chatting with Chase and Nolan, already chugging from a red Solo cup. I know I should join him, but the idea of it exhausts me. Without meaning to, I find my gaze slipping back to the tree I'd seen Christian under. He's still going at it with the dark-haired girl, and I feel sick. Maybe I shouldn't have offered to be the DD. I could really use a drink tonight. Watching Christian stick his tongue down another girl's throat makes me want to get so drunk I can't think straight. But I know better. My parents have scared me with their endless stories of people wrapping their cars around trees or killing poor innocent families while driving drunk. It's not a risk

I'm willing to take. Besides, drinking has never appealed to me. In all the times I've watched Ashley get hammered, nothing about it has appeared fun. The first time I saw her fall all over herself and puke in the bushes, I decided the party life wasn't for me.

Pulling my gaze away from Christian, I hurry over to Josh. Perhaps if I focus on my boyfriend I can erase all thoughts of the boy that shouldn't be on my mind. As Josh drapes his arm over my shoulders, drawing me into his side, I remind myself that I made the right choice when I stayed with him. Clearly our kiss meant nothing to Christian. He kisses new girls every week. It's like his lips can't help themselves. They have to attach to any girl within a two-mile radius or something. I can't believe I fell for his act. I would've thrown away everything for him, and that would have been the worst mistake ever.

Then I would be alone right now. My stomach clenches at the thought. There's nothing I hate more than being alone. My mom loves solitude. I've heard her say a million times that her favorite part of the day is when we are at school and she has the house to herself. Which I guess makes sense because that's when she gets to spend time with imaginary characters, and we all know that she likes them more than real-life people. As a kid I used to be so jealous of her characters. In her office she has a corkboard where she pins little index cards filled with information about her characters – height, weight, hair and eye color. I used to go into her office, yank down those cards and tear them into tiny pieces. It was like I believed I could truly get rid of them that way. But all I succeeded in doing was making Mom upset with me. As if I needed to give her any more ammunition.

But I don't have imaginary friends or characters filling my mind. Therefore, when I'm alone, I'm truly alone. And I hate it. I hate the silence. I hate the emptiness. I hate the loneliness. But most of all I hate feeling like no one really cares. Being at this party with Josh's arm around me, I can pretend I'm someone special. Someone worthy of attention. Even if deep down, I know it isn't true.

Josh, Chase and Nolan are talking about baseball while chugging their beers. The bitter scent wafts under my nose. When Josh laughs some beer sloughs out of his cup and lands on the toe of my boot. He doesn't notice and keeps on talking. Ashley sidles up beside me, her gaze flitting around. Clearly she's on the prowl. I nod my head in Hayes' direction.

"Hayes has been checkin' you out since we got here," I say.

"Of course he has." She rolls her eyes. "But I'm so not interested."

"Why not? Hayes is a nice guy." I've always liked him. He's funny and easy to talk to. He never judges me the way some of the other guys do. During the first baseball party I attended with Ashley, he was the only guy who talked to me at all. Ashley had immediately abandoned me for some guy she hooked up with, and I was all by myself. None of the other guys on the team would even look at me, much less talk to me. *Oh, the perils of being the pitcher's sister.* But Hayes saw me sitting alone in the middle of the field counting weeds, and we struck up a conversation. By the end of the night I found myself crushing on him a little. Cal was upset when he found us, worried that Hayes had been hitting on me, but I assured him that Hayes wasn't. And I was being truthful. Nothing about the way Hayes interacted with me felt predatory at all. He was nice, friendly, and funny. That's it.

"I'm not looking for nice." Ashley stares at Hayes, wrinkling her nose. "I'm looking for hot. And that tub o' goo is not hot."

I hate when Ashley says things like that. Hayes is a bigger guy, yes. But he's not fat. Not even a little bit. And he may not be hot in the standard sense of the word, but he is good looking. Not in the way Christian or Josh is, but I still think he's cute. Besides, doesn't personality count for anything anymore? The truth is that there are times I wish I'd ended up dating Hayes instead of Josh. I'd probably be happier.

My gaze involuntarily skates over to Christian as if it has a mind of its own. And I realize that Hayes wouldn't actually make me happy either. There's only one guy I really want to be with, and he's currently in the arms of another girl.

"Hey, what's going on with you?" Ashley asks, her eyes following mine.

"Nothing." I shake my head vehemently.

She knits her eyebrows together. "You sure?"

"Positive." Man, I need to stop staring at Christian. I'm making everyone suspicious.

Ashley's mouth drops open. "Is that your brother?"

My head whips to where she's looking. "Oh, no." I've never seen my brother so drunk. He can barely walk. He's stumbling over his own feet while some girl tries and fails to hold him up. But that doesn't stop him from laughing and hollering out unintelligible things. Even though I promised myself I wouldn't look at Christian anymore tonight, I have no choice. He's the only one who can help me right now.

Lucky for me, he's finally stopped kissing that girl. And that's when I recognize her as Selena,

151

one of the softball players. *Great.* There's no way I can compete with her. It was the main reason I wanted to play ball when I was younger – so I'd have something in common with Christian and Cal. Seems that Selena has an advantage I can only dream of. Cal's laughing catches my attention, reminding me that there's something more important I have to deal with right now.

"Um…Josh. I'll be right back." I nod my head toward Cal. "I have to go deal with…something."

He nods with understanding, yet there is a flicker of annoyance in his eyes. I can't worry about it right now though. Stepping away from him, I head toward my brother. The ground slopes downward and I lose my footing, my ankle rolling to the side slightly. *Geez, I haven't even been drinking.* Cheeks warming, I hope no one noticed. Regaining my balance, I hurry forward. Christian catches my eye and moves toward us.

"Hey," Cal slurs when I approach. "What are you doing here, lil sis?"

"Hey, man," Christian cuts in. Looking over

at the girl trying to hold Cal up, he smiles. "Thanks. We'll take it from here."

Relief passes over her features when Christian grabs Cal's arm, drawing him away from the girl.

"What's up, man?" Cal says to Christian.

"Nothing much. Seems my night isn't as interesting as yours." A look of amusement passes over his features. He hoists Cal up, holding him under one armpit. "Emmy, can you grab his other side?"

"Sure." I do as I'm told.

"Emmy?" Cal looks bewildered as if he's seeing me for the first time.

I shake my head.

Christian ignores his comment. "C'mon, Cal. Let's get you home."

"But I don't wanna go home. I'm having fun." Cal pouts.

"What the hell is wrong with him?" I hiss. My brother isn't a huge partier. Sure, he likes going to parties, but he rarely drinks, and never like this.

"He and Melissa broke up," Christian
153

explains as we walk forward.

"Melissa," Cal says her name with disgust.

"Ah, I see." My heart goes out to my brother. I know what it feels like to lose someone you care about. I glance at Christian as we drag Cal toward where the cars are parked in the gravel. Not that I've lost Christian. He's right here. But he's not mine.

He never has been.

And probably never will be.

It's a depressing thought, and I understand my brother's need to drink. To forget. To be numb. The problem is that eventually he'll have to wake up. He'll have to face everything again, and I already feel sorry for when that happens.

When we reach Christian's car, he opens the passenger side door and we guide Cal inside. Once we shut the door, Cal leans his face against the window, his cheek pressed against the glass. I'm sure he'll be fast asleep by the time Christian pulls out of here.

"Thanks," I say. Awkwardness hangs between us.

"Of course. I'm happy to help." He smiles.

"Sorry I had to tear you away from Selena. Seems like the two of you were having a good time."

I may be imagining it, but I swear I see shame cross his features. But then he shrugs. "It's okay. Cal needed me."

I glance at the car. Cal's eyes are closed, his mouth gaping open. "Think he'll be okay?"

"You mean from the hangover or the break up?"

"Both, I guess."

"I think he'll have a rough day tomorrow and then he'll feel better. But it might be a little while before he gets over Melissa." His eyes crash into mine. "It's hard to get over someone when you really like them."

I swallow hard. "Yeah, it is."

"You want me to give you a ride too? I am going by your house, after all."

"Um…no. I better stay."

He shifts uncomfortably from one foot to the other. "Right. Well, you better get back to your boyfriend before he starts to worry."

I hate the sarcastic way he says the word "boyfriend." Frankly, I hate this whole awkward conversation. It's not the way I want things to be between us. "Yeah," I practically whisper.

A breeze fans over me, and I shiver. Christian starts to reach for me, but then pulls back. "You should have worn a jacket. That little dress is not gonna keep you warm tonight."

"It's Ashley's," I say, and then wonder why I feel the need to clarify.

He pauses, looking me over. "You look pretty." My heart skips a beat, my cheeks warming. Clearing his throat, he adds, "Well, maybe you should see if Josh will let you wear his jacket." He averts his gaze. "I better get Cal home."

When he walks to the driver's side, desperation blooms inside of me like a flower opening up. I want nothing more than to jump in the car. Riding home with Cal and Christian sounds so much better than watching Josh and Ashley get drunk all night and then driving them home. But I have to stay. I'm their ride.

As Christian drives away, my stomach drops. For several minutes I watch the headlights of his car as he guides it down the road. Once it's out of sight, I take a few deep breaths. Then I trudge back to the party, dread descending on me.

My heart is somewhere on the back roads driving toward my house.

"Emmy." A dark figure steps out from behind the trees.

I gasp, clutching my chest. "Josh," I breathe out. "You scared me." My heart thumps beneath my palms, reminding me of a frantic drumbeat, of that dubstep music Cal sometimes listens to. I take deep breaths in an effort to return it to its normal cadence. One. Two. Three.

"Everything okay with Cal?" He steps toward me, cupping my elbow with his hand. I want to think of it as a protective gesture, but it feels different. More like a gesture of ownership.

"Yeah." I nod.

"What about Christian?"

My throat feels dry. "Um…yeah. But, I mean, I don't even think he'd been drinking."

"That's not what I meant." His tone hardens.

My chest tightens. "W-what did you mean?"

"You tell me."

"Huh?" *Crap. Does he know something?* My head spins.

"Em, is there something going on with you and Christian?"

Now is the perfect time to spill my guts. I can tell him everything and then wash my hands of the whole thing. Then maybe it won't have this hold on me. Perhaps then I can let it go. I can release its power.

Only I know it's not that simple. If I confess it to Josh it will open up a whole new can of worms. Besides, the season is starting soon. I won't have it be my fault that there's contention amongst the team. Sure, Christian and Josh don't like each other, but I have no doubt they'll find a way to work together on the field. Mostly because Christian is a professional. He doesn't let his feelings rule the way he plays. And it's his senior year. He's going away to college next year to play ball. No way will he risk screwing anything up this season. However, if Josh finds out about Christian and me he won't be able to let it go. I know Josh. Once he's angry he can't control his emotions. Not on or off the field.

Saying something now will not only blow my life apart, but Christian's too. And I won't do that. Not even to clear my guilty conscious.

"Nope. Nothing," I say with a smile. Then I lean in and softly kiss him on the lips. "We're just friends, that's all."

"Okay." Josh kisses me back. I can't tell if he believes me or not, but I go with it, hoping my kiss will convince him.

He's been drinking so his kiss is sloppy, his hands roaming freely down to the hem of my dress. I want to push his hands away, but I know better. Now is not the time. It will only make him suspicious.

"Man, baby, have I told you how hot you look tonight?" Rank, beer-scented breath blows over my cheek.

I used to love when Josh called me hot. It

made me feel special. But for some reason tonight it turns my stomach. I think back to when Christian called me pretty. It meant more to me than all of the times Josh has called me hot. Once again, my mind travels back to Christian's car, and I can't help but feel like that's where I belong.

CHRISTIAN

Cal is on fire tonight. Too bad I'm not.

It's our first scrimmage, and we're playing our rival team. Every time I fail to block the ball I tell myself it doesn't matter; that it's not a real game. But that's bull, and I know it. Even scrimmages count. At least in my mind. Every time I play it matters. I need to be on my game. Especially this year – my final year playing in high school. It's a big deal. And I can't afford to play like crap.

After the first inning, Cal intercepts me on the way to the dugout.

"What's up with you tonight?" He clamps a hand on my shoulder.

"Nothing," I answer quickly. "Just having

an off night, I guess."

"Well, get back on. I need you out there."

"Yeah, I know." I drum up a smile I don't feel. Once we sit in the dugout, my gaze travels out to the bleachers. Emmy sits right in the front row, her hand halfway inside a bag of Doritos. After pulling one out, she chomps down on it. Orange residue coats her bottom lip and she reaches up to wipe if off. I wish I was sitting there. I'd gladly do that for her. Shaking away the thought, I glance over at Selena, sitting a few rows up. Her eyes are intently watching the game, her body rigid as she sits forward. My heart pinches.

I never should've started anything up with her. She's a great girl. Hot, easy to be around, great ball player. She's exactly the kind of girl I normally go for. But the timing's not right. I'm only using her to get my mind off of Emmy. If it were anyone else it might be okay, but it feels wrong to do it to her. It's obvious she really likes me. When we were talking on the phone last night she pretty much admitted that she's had a crush on me for awhile.

I'm ashamed to admit that my first thought

was that it was perfect. She's the perfect distraction. And maybe if I tried hard enough she could be the perfect replacement. But as I've thought about it, it's become crystal clear that it won't work. Emmy is not a broken dish. She's a person. And no one can replace her.

I'm hoping one day I'll meet someone who overshadows her. Someone I like even more than Emmy. But not a replacement.

There's no way I can replace years of conversations and moments. Years of games and laughter. It can't be done. But one thing is clear. Until I can get over her, it's not fair to string anyone else along.

"Ya feeling okay, Cal?" Josh sits down on the bench on the other side of Cal.

Cal gives him a funny look. "I'd say by the way I'm playing that I must feel pretty damn good. Which is more than I can say for you, Joshy."

There is a collective round of "ooohs" around us.

My lips twitch at the corners. Cal and I exchange fist bumps.

Josh's face reddens, but he recovers quickly, honing in on me. "Then I guess you're the one who's not feeling well."

I shake my head. "Maybe you wouldn't suck so bad if you spent more time worrying about yourself, Easton." I purposefully use his last name because I know it will bother him. The last person he wants commenting about his family is me.

"I think it's time you took your own advice, Alcott." When he throws my last name back in my face, his gaze flickers over to the stands, landing on my mom.

"Trust me, I don't worry about you at all," I snap.

"No, but you spend a lot of time worrying about my girlfriend."

Now he's gone too far. Cal's head spins in his direction.

"Hey, that's my sister you're talking about, dick. And she's a lot more our responsibility than yours."

Josh backs down after that, and it causes a smile to break out on my face. *That's right. Be careful who you mess with, little boy.*

When it's time for us to take the field, I purposefully ram my shoulder into Josh's as we pass. When he throws me a disgusted look, I smile back. But when I glance at the bleachers to see Emmy staring adoringly in Josh's direction my stomach sours. Crouching, I get into position and try to focus on the game, but it's no use. Emmy's stupid expression is burned into my brain.

This is going to be a long game.

****

When the game ends, I feel nothing but relief. We did end up winning, no thanks to me. Luckily, Cal pulled us through. And I'm hoping I can get it together by the next time I play. After getting a tongue lashing by Coach Hopkins, I trudge off the field, my bat bag slung over my shoulder. The gear clangs around inside, shifting with each step. The first person I see is Selena. She smiles and stands when I approach, as if she's been waiting for me.

"You did great," she says.

"No, I didn't."

"Okay, you didn't." She flashes me an apologetic grin. "But the team did."

"Yeah," I agree.

"And you'll do better next time."

"Yeah, I will." I suck in a breath, gathering courage. *It's now or never.* My only hope of getting my game up is to be honest with her. "Look, Selena, I think you're really cool, but…it's just…" *Damn it, I'm never good at this part.*

She throws up her hand to stop me. "It's okay. I won't make you go through with the entire speech. I know exactly where this is going."

"You do?" I raise one eyebrow.

She nods. "And it's okay. We're not even really dating. You don't have to hurt yourself by coming up with some long, break-up speech."

The fact that she's being so cool about this makes it even harder. "I'm sorry." Man, I feel like crap.

"You're really cool too, Christian," she says. "I had a lot of fun with you this weekend, and I think we could have had a lot of fun in the future."

166

She studies me a minute. "You're a good guy and, for your sake, I hope she feels the same way you do."

"Who?" My heart freezes.

She shrugs. "The girl you're in love with."

"I'm not in love with anyone." *Am I?*

"Hmmm. Usually I'm so good at reading these things." She furrows her brows. "But there is someone else, right? That's why you're breaking it off with me?"

I nod. No sense in denying it now.

"I hope it works out for you." With one last sad smile, she squeezes my arm and then walks off leaving me a clear view of Emmy. She's sitting alone, her gaze fixated on me. I start to wonder where Josh is, but then dismiss the thought. I don't want to think about him right now. Smiling, I take a few steps forward. When Emmy stands to greet me, my heart arrests. Suddenly nothing about tonight matters. Not how crappy I played in the scrimmage or the fact that I might have just broken some poor girl's heart. All that matters is this moment. And in this moment everything feels right. It's amazing how simply being in Emmy's presence calms me. I wonder about Selena's words. Is this what love feels like?

Do I love Emmy?

EMMY

I know I should be focused on Josh. He's who I came here to watch. I mean, other than Cal. But the truth is that I'm not watching either of them. It's like Christian has a target painted on him or something. Or like my eyes are magnets and he's the fridge. I can't stop staring at him the entire game. He's not playing as well as he normally does, and I know it must be killing him. Even when he and Cal were little kids he was so hard on himself when he didn't play well. They both were.

There was one particularly bad game when they were around ten or eleven. Christian couldn't make a single catch. It's like he had oil in his glove or something. I remember thinking that at the time, and I knew it was funny. So funny that if I had said it about anyone else Cal and Christian would have laughed. But I knew better than to share it with them that day.

Christian came over to our house after the game because his mom was busy at the shop. He tried to act tough, but I could see the tears in his eyes when he thought no one was looking. I didn't know what to do, but I wanted to comfort him so badly. Mom had made chocolate chip cookies earlier that day, and I knew they were Christian's favorite. So I heated one up for him, making it all gooey the way he liked. Then I brought it to him in the family room where he and Cal were playing video games. Cal got upset with me for not bringing him a cookie, but Christian smiled knowingly and whispered "thank you" so softly that only I could hear.

Today I long to comfort him the same way I did all those years ago. The problem is that I don't think a cookie will do the trick this time.

After the game I wait while Coach Hopkins talks to the team. The bleachers clear out, most of the spectators leaving. But there are still stragglers. Most of us are the players' girlfriends. Irrational annoyance rises in me at the fact that one of them is Selena. I had figured that what happened between Christian and Selena at the party was nothing more than a random hookup, but now it seems it's more than that. It shouldn't bother me since I'm with Josh anyway, but it does.

After the coach is finished, the players disperse, many of them heading in our direction. The minute Josh comes out, my insides coil. He played worse than Christian, and if his facial expression is any indicator he's pretty pissed about it.

"Hey," he says gruffly when he approaches me.

"Hey," I respond. For a minute I contemplate offering him platitudes, but decide against it. He knows he played crappy. No sense in humoring him.

"Look, I know we were supposed to hang out tonight, but I'm not in the mood."

Shame washes over me at how relieved I feel. "No worries. I get it."

"Call me later?"

171

"Sure."

He gives me a half-hearted peck on the cheek and then takes off. I almost leave too, but then I see Christian saying goodbye to Selena. Freezing, I watch them. She touches his arm and walks away. No kiss. No hug. Narrowing my eyes, I wonder what's going on with them. Once she's gone, his head bobs up, his eyes meeting mine. Without a word, he steps toward me. I stand, and offer him a small smile.

"You okay?" I ask.

"A little better now."

"Because of Selena?" I have to know.

He shakes his head. "There's nothing going on there."

"Didn't look like that on Saturday night."

"That was a mistake," he says, and I'm reminded of his words after our kiss. Seems he's full of mistakes.

But I don't want to rehash all of that right now. I want to go back to when things were normal between us. "Too bad I don't have any cookies."

He chuckles. "Yeah, no kidding. I could

really use one right about now."

****

It's Friday night, and it's pouring down rain. Water is coming down fiercely past my window. Grey clouds cover the sky making it pitch dark outside. Ashley groans and flings her back down on the bed. In her hand she holds her phone, her gaze glued to the screen.

"Looks like the party has been canceled," she whines.

"Of course. Where would they have it?" I glance out my window, at the liquid splattering it. Above us it sounds like waves crashing over the roof of my house. "It's not like they could have it at Old Willis's farm. The wood slats in the barn wouldn't keep anyone dry."

"What are we gonna do now?" Ashley rolls over onto her stomach, propping her elbows up on the bed and lowering her chin into her palms.

"I guess we could have the sleepover you told your parents we were having." I raise my eyebrows. Ashley's parents are much stricter than mine. Her dad is a doctor and her mom stays home. They don't let her go to parties or date boys. That's where I come in. I swear, Ashley's parents must think that she and I spend every waking moment together. Whenever she's at a party or out with a boy they think she's at my house. Sometimes it isn't exactly a lie. Take tonight, for instance. We were planning on going to the party, but then we were coming back to my house afterward. So technically she was always planning on a sleepover at my house.

My parents, on the other hand, are pretty lax. They let me go to parties as long as I don't drink and drive. Really they don't want me drinking at all, but they're not naïve enough to think it will never happen. Both of my parents partied a lot when they were younger, so it's like they think it's a rite of passage or something. Plus, it helps that I have Cal looking out for me. I think that gives them some peace of mind.

"Yeah, I guess." Ashley sighs.

Clearly she's bummed, but honestly I'm glad

the party got canceled. I'm tired of going to parties. There was a time when I would have given my right arm to be invited to one of the baseball team parties. But now that I've gone to a few, I'm kind of over it. I suppose if I liked to drink like Ashley does it would be more fun. But for me it's a long night of hanging outside in the cold watching people act like idiots. A night in the comfort of my own home sounds so much better.

"It'll be fun," I assure her. "We can watch movies and eat popcorn."

"Cause that's what I need. Popcorn." She rolls over and pinches at her taut stomach.

"Oh, shut up. There's not an ounce of fat on your body."

"Yes, there is. See." She grips at her skin.

"You're crazy. But it's fine if you don't want popcorn. I won't make any." This is the reason I like hanging out with Cal and Chris. They inhale food. They never worry about gaining weight, and they never judge me for eating. "I'll just grab us some drinks."

This perks her up. "Alcoholic drinks?"

I shake my head. "My parents are cool, but they're not that cool." I glance outside and shiver. "I can make us hot chocolate."

"Yuck." She makes a face.

"Soda?"

"Okay." She nods.

"I'll be right back." I slide off my bed and walk out into the hallway. My feet sink into the plush carpet as I walk. When I enter the kitchen, Cal is standing in front of the open fridge, and Christian is sitting on a barstool. I hadn't even realized Christian was here.

"There's nothing to eat." Cal slams the fridge door shut.

"Let's go grab some burgers then," Christian responds.

Cal turns around, and I walk forward. "Oh, hey, Em. Wanna come with us to grab some food?"

"Out into the storm?" I cock an eyebrow. "I don't think so. Besides, Ashley's here and she's not really eating tonight."

Cal chuckles.

Christian shakes his head. "We'll get you

something."

I toss him a look of gratitude. "Thanks." *Screw Ashley.* I can always eat.

Christian jumps down from the barstool, and Cal scoops his keys off the counter.

"See ya in a few," Cal says.

"Be careful out there," I warn him.

"Yes, Mom," he jokes back.

"Mom wouldn't say that," I point out.

"True." Cal smiles.

"She might," Christian interjects, "if one of her characters recently got into an accident during a storm."

Cal and I both laugh. Nobody else outside of this family understands my mom as well as Christian. As they head outside, I open the fridge and pull out two sodas. When I whirl around, a gasp sounds at the back of my throat.

"Ashley! I didn't even hear you come in here."

"That's because you were preoccupied." Leaning against the kitchen doorway, she wears a funny expression. One that makes me feel scrutinized and exposed.

"Here." Holding out one of the sodas, I make my way toward her.

She takes the can in her hand and pops the top. It fizzes. With her gaze still trained on me, she takes a sip. Then she lowers the soda and cocks her head to the side. "So, are you ever gonna tell me what's going on?"

I almost spew soda out of my mouth. "With what?"

"With you, silly?" She says with a smile. "C'mon, I'm your best friend. I can tell something's up. You've been acting really strange lately."

"I have?" If that's true, has everyone noticed it?

She nods. "I mean, you used to like Josh so much, and lately you act like you don't like him at all. And you've been acting super strange around Christian. It doesn't take a rocket scientist to figure out something happened there."

Apparently not if Ashley picked up on it. I blow out a resigned breath. "Fine. I'll tell you, but you have to swear never to tell a single soul."

"I swear." She holds up her free hand, as if she's taking a pledge.

I bite my lip, still unsure if I can tell her.

"Em, I'm your best friend. You can trust me."

She's right. She *is* my best friend. So then why am I so reluctant to share this with her? Maybe because once I say the words aloud it will make it real, but I suspect it's more than that. I don't share secrets with Ashley. I've always had Cal and Christian for that. It's weird to admit that I trust Christian more than I do Ashley, but it's the truth. In fact, I trust Christian more than I trust almost anyone else. And right now he's the only person who knows what happened between us. Do I want someone else to know?

"Seriously. It must be really bad if you can't even tell me." Ashley frowns.

My stomach knots. At this point what she's thinking is probably worse. "No, it's not that bad."

Giggling reaches my ears, traveling from my parents' room. Canned television laughter follows.

One thing I do know is that I can't risk my

parents hearing this. "Let's go into my room, and then I'll tell you."

Ashley nods, her eyes lighting up. It makes me feel a little sick. Gossip is something Ashley loves. I can't believe I'm going to spill this information to her. As I follow her back to my room, I silently pray that I'm not making a huge mistake.

Holding our sodas, we plop down on my bed.

"You promise you won't tell a single soul?"

Ashley lets out an exasperated groan. "I already promised. Don't you trust me?"

I don't dare answer that.

Hurt flashes in her eyes. "I tell you everything, don't I?"

"Yeah?" It ends up sounding like a question because I'm not sure. She does tell me a lot, but I have no idea if it's everything.

"Yes, because that's what best friends do." She flips a strand of hair over her shoulder. "I mean, if you can't trust your best friend, who can you trust?"

She does have a point. "Okay, I'll tell you." I take another gulp of my soda as if that will give me a boost of bravery. Once I swallow it, I glance up at Ashley. "Remember the night of the bonfire party?"

"When you and Josh broke up?"

"Yeah," I say. "Well, Christian gave us a ride home, remember?"

Ashley giggles. "I don't remember much of that night, but yeah, kind of."

"Yeah, no kidding." I smile. "Anyway, when we got back to my house we talked for a little while. He was sort of comforting me, trying to make me feel better about my fight with Josh. And then he…" I pause, taking a deep breath.

"He what?" Ashley leans forward.

"He sort of kissed me."

"What?" She jerks her arm and a little soda spills out on my bedspread.

I throw her a stern look.

"Sorry." She sets her soda down on my nightstand, grabs a kleenex and cleans up her spill. When she peers up at me, her eyes are wide. "Does

181

Cal know?"

"No." I'm surprised that he's the first person she asked about. "And he's never going to find out."

"Good plan, because he'd totally freak out."

"I know," I say. "That's why I haven't said anything."

Ashley purses her lips. "So it was just a one-time thing, then?"

I hesitate, and she catches it.

"You want it to happen again, don't you?"

"It doesn't matter. It's not going to."

"Why not? If you like him, you have to go for it, Emmy. To hell with your brother."

"He's not the only factor here," I point out.

Ashley's eyebrows knit together. "Oh, yeah. You mean Josh."

I actually hadn't thought of Josh at all, but I nod anyway.

She waves away my words. "Oh, come on. It's not like you're married. You're only sixteen. Now's the time to have fun."

"It's not that simple, Ash." I pick at my

comforter with my fingernails. "Christian's like family. It was a mistake. It happened, but now it's over."

My head snaps up at the sound of the front door opening and closing. Christian and Cal's loud chattering reaches my ears. I stiffen as footsteps head down the hallway. There's knocking on my bedroom door, and I hurry to answer it. Christian stands in my doorway, his hair damp, his face red from the cold.

"Here you are." He holds up a white paper bag. I inhale the scent of grease and hamburgers. "No onion or mayo. Just the way you like it." A smile spreads across his face.

I take the bag in between my fingers. It crinkles upon contact.

"We got a hamburger for Miss Anorexic over there too." Christian looks past my shoulder.

Ashley curls her nose in disgust. "No, thank you."

Christian shrugs. "More for us then."

"Thanks." I grin, my stomach growling. After shutting my bedroom door, I turn around.

183

Trust me, it's not over," Ashley says, a knowing smile on her face.

"What?"

"There is some major tension between the two of you."

I shush her. "Keep your voice down, Ash."

"Fine, but I'm telling you that boy still wants you."

I mull over her words, wondering if she's right. The scary part is that I desperately want it to be true.

CHRISTIAN

The rain hasn't let up all weekend. By Sunday afternoon, I'm sick of it. On the news they keep saying how great it is since we need the rain. And it's true that we've been in a drought. Logically, I know I should be happy. Only I can't be happy because I can't do the one thing that makes me happy – play ball. I've been stuck inside for days, and I'm going stir crazy.

Lying on my couch, television blaring in the background, I text Cal to see if he wants to go see a movie or something. But he texts back to say that he's working on a paper for English. All of my homework is finished. Man, how lame is it that I want to do homework?

However, I'd do almost anything to get my mind off of Emmy. The more I stay inside, the more she consumes my thoughts. Especially after spending the night at Cal's on Friday night. It was torture to sleep on the couch knowing that Emmy was merely down the hallway. All I had to do was walk a few feet and I could be next to her. It took all the self-control I possess not to test it; not to try to touch her or kiss her again. It drove me mad.

Today I've been trying to watch movies to get my mind off of her, but that hasn't worked at all. I'm pretty sure baseball is the only thing that could preoccupy me, but the rain has taken that option away. Therefore, I need to come up with a new plan. Sitting around thinking about her isn't helping me at all.

I can't have her.

It's as simple as that.

Now if only I could get that through my thick skull and quit hoping for something more.

Standing, I decide to head down to the shop and check on Mom. She didn't have any shipments this weekend, so there probably won't be anything for me to do. But being there sure beats sitting around here feeling sorry for myself. After putting on my shoes and jacket, I grab my car keys and head out the front door. Bitter cold stings my face as wind whips rain into my eyes. I pull my hood over my head, cinch it tight and run to my car. By the time I reach it, I'm soaked. My clothes cling to my body, and I shiver. Once inside, rain pelts the roof of my car. It's louder than the engine. I turn the wipers on full blast so I can see. Still, liquid splatters the windshield as I pull away from the curb.

I drive slowly into Old Towne, and park directly in front of the shop. It's not a good sign that parking is available. My gaze sweeps the street when I step out of the car. It's pretty empty. Then again, it's not exactly shopping weather. Most people are probably holed up in their homes or sitting in the movie theatre. Any activity that keeps them dry. It's not like you could even call this a real storm, but it's about as bad as gets around here. We don't get extreme weather. The only storms I've ever seen are in the movies. Rain and wind are about the worst we experience.

Slamming my car door closed I make a run

for it, shielding my face with my arm. The bell on the door dings when I step inside the shop. I yank off my hood and shake my head. Water drops from my body onto the musty carpet. I wipe my feet and step forward. That's when I hear voices further back in the shop. I'm surprised. Maybe Mom does have a customer after all.

I walk forward, curious about the person who braved the elements to go to an antique shop. My feet shuffle on the ground with every step, my elbows brushing lamp shades and furniture. Mom has so much stuff crammed in here that the aisles are pretty narrow. I imagine if a person was claustrophobic they wouldn't be able to shop here. Often I've tried to push things back, to allow more room, but then we get more stuff and the aisles end up like this again. Dust tickles my nose, and I have the urge to sneeze. But then it passes.

I round a corner and that's when I spot him. I freeze, the hairs on the back of my neck prickling. He and my mom stop talking, both of them turning in my direction.

"Chris, I didn't know you were coming by,"

Mom says, seemingly unfazed.

If only I could feel the same way, but I don't. My pulse races, my head spinning. I breathe in deeply through my nose and exhale through my mouth in an effort to calm the hell down. Mom will not be happy if I lose it. "Thought I'd come by to see if you needed any help, but clearly you don't." I look pointedly at Mr. Easton. *Seriously, what the hell is he doing here?*

"Dan came by to pick up a gift for his mom. She's always loved antiques," Mom answers my silent question as if she read my mind.

But it's his name that sticks out to me. The way she speaks it with such ease. I wasn't aware they spoke at all. Has she forgotten everything he's done to her?

"Hi, Christian." He steps forward, offering his hand. "It's good to see you again."

Narrowing my eyes, I stare down at his hand. Mom clears her throat, a demand. Obediently, I shake Mr. Easton's hand. It's cold and clammy to the touch. I feel disgusted.

"Enjoyed the scrimmage the other day," he

says.

I scowl. "Wasn't exactly my best game." Is that what he wants from me? To grovel? To admit my shortcomings?

"It wasn't my son's best game either," he says. "But you guys will get it together by the time the season starts."

I'm stunned by his words. I wonder what Josh would think about his dad throwing him under the bus like that? As much as I can't stand the kid, I feel kind of bad for him. No one wants to be criticized by their old man. Then again, I'd take criticism from mine. Hell, I'd take anything from mine.

"I'll go ahead and wrap this up for you." Mom carries an antique bowl toward the register.

Not wanting to get stuck talking to Mr. Easton any longer, I follow her. While she rings up his purchase, I stand off to the side watching. Their conversation is stilted, awkward, exactly like I'd imagine it should be. However, it's not at all how it sounded when I first arrived, and suspicions arise.

"See you two later," Mr. Easton says as he

makes his way to the door, bag in hand.

"Bye, Dan," Mom calls after him.

I force a nod, but keep my lips tightly closed. Once he's gone I turn a challenging gaze to Mom. "What was that all about?"

"What?" She shrugs. "I made a sale. And just in time too. This day was turning out to be a bust. I seriously couldn't spend one more second staring outside at the depressing rain."

She's saying too much. That's what people do when they're nervous or lying. They keep talking. They can't shut up.

"I thought you hated each other," I state.

Sighing, she runs her fingers through her hair. Today she's wearing it down, and it's loose around her shoulders. Rarely does she wear it that way, but when she does I think it makes her look younger. "I've never hated him."

"But he hated you."

"Probably." She nods. "And he had every right to. But that was a long time ago. I'd like to think we've both matured since then."

"So you're friends now?" *Unbelievable.*

Mom bristles. "Watch the tone, Chris."

"This is crazy. You're in here chatting it up with him, and you're telling me to watch my tone." Anger claws at me.

Mom steps out from behind the counter, her expression hard. "Need I remind you that I'm your mom? I know it's always been the two of us, and sometimes you forget your role, but you're my son. I don't have to explain myself to you."

Taking a step back, I recoil from her words. My mom has always demanded respect, but it's rare that she talks to me like this. "So that's it, then? You're gonna just keep hanging out with the guy?"

"C'mon, Chris. Don't make this into a big deal. He came to buy his mom a gift. Sometimes he does that." She smiles at me. "Okay?"

"I'm sorry," I mutter, feeling like an ass. "I just don't want to see you get hurt again."

"I appreciate that," Mom says. "But you have to trust me. I know what I'm doing."

****

My attraction to Emmy terrified me from the beginning. From the first day when I saw her in that damn red bikini. I was terrified of Cal finding out. Terrified I wouldn't be able to hide my feelings. But mostly, terrified of having to watch her date someone else.

Emmy never dated. Unless you counted Miles in middle school, but I didn't. I knew she never liked that guy. Emmy kept to herself, finding solace in school work and numbers. So I had hoped there was nothing to worry about. But then she started tagging along to the baseball parties with Ashley. That was when fear took root for me. Emmy dating anyone would be awful. Emmy dating a guy on my team would be hell.

Luckily none of the guys went after her. I had Cal to thank for that. None of the guys wanted to chance pissing off our star pitcher by hitting on his little sister. There was one party where Hayes talked to her for awhile, but Cal assured me that Hayes hadn't come on to her. I was sure he wanted to, but I knew he'd never compromise his standing with Cal. As days passed, my chest expanded a little, my worry dissipating. I thought I was home free. I figured by the time Emmy dated someone I'd be away at college and wouldn't have to witness it.

But then the unthinkable happened.

It was a random weekday. It started out like all the others. I dragged my sorry ass out of bed and went to school. Had I known what I was about to encounter, I might have stayed home. Stayed tucked into my warm covers, perhaps for all of eternity. But I didn't. I marched right into the school hallway, a book tucked under my arm, my backpack strapped on my back. And that's when I saw them – Emmy and Josh – lip-locked at his locker.

I almost dropped my book. I almost threw my backpack. I almost hit the guy in his face.

However, I knew I couldn't do any of those things. Mainly because it would be irrational. I had no claim to Emmy. She was free to date whomever she wanted. Even though I wanted her to be with me, I knew that would be impossible.

But none of these rational thoughts made it any easier to see her with him.

And to this day, it hasn't gotten any better. I

still cringe when I pass them in the halls. My stomach still knots when I catch them kissing or holding hands. I still fantasize about punching him in the face about a million times a day.

And it's only gotten worse since the night we kissed. Not just because of the way he treated her, but because that kiss ignited my feelings. It made the small spark of attraction I felt for her grow into a full-blown flame. And pretty soon I fear it will singe everything in sight.

Ever since Emmy and Josh have gotten back together, I've been watching him closely. No way am I going to let him get away with treating her the way he did at the bonfire party. And so far he's been pretty cool. He wants everyone to believe he's turned over a new leaf or something, but I know better.

The guy's a dick. He always has been, and always will be. No matter what others believe, I'm not falling for his act. Not for a minute. It's also why I'm not surprised when I catch him flirting with another girl in the hall before third period.

Regardless, I'm not letting him get away

with it.

He's leaning against the locker, all smiles and raised eyebrows, when I approach. His grin falters a bit when he spots me.

"What's up, Joshy," I say in my best condescending tone.

The smile on his face slips further. "Nothin' much," he speaks with an irritated edge to his tone.

"Who's this?" I indicate the petite blond he's talking to.

"None of your business," he sneers.

"Really?" I raise my brows. "Well, then you won't mind if I tell Emmy about her."

His tone hardens. "Go ahead. She's no one. Just a friend."

The girl's face falls, and I feel kind of bad for her. But only kind of. Truth is, I've done her a favor. Shaking her head, she stalks off.

"What's your problem, man?" Josh narrows his eyes at me.

"You're my problem."

Josh laughs. "Damn, you're like a walking cliché, you know that? Like a character on one of those teen sitcoms, but not nearly as witty."

"If we are on one of those shows, then I guess that makes you the expendable guy. The one who's not needed. The one no one likes."

"Oh, I think you've got that backwards." he says. "By the way, how is your dad, Chris?"

"Watch it." I grit my teeth, tired of his smart-ass comments. Tired of his crap. Tired of him. Reaching out, I grab the collar of his shirt and slam him up against the locker.

"Whoa." He throws up his arms, glancing around at the crowded halls. "You're not gonna throw down with me right here, are you? What would happen to our star pitcher if his favorite catcher got benched?"

I hate that he's right. Grunting, I release my grip on him. "We certainly wouldn't miss your sorry ass if you were out."

He squints as if scrutinizing me, and steps closer. "What's your real issue with me, Chris?"

"I want you out of Emmy's life." *There. I said it.*

"Too bad it's not your call, man." A small

smile spreads across his face. "It's Emmy's. And let me tell you, right now she's calling all day long."

It's sick what he's insinuating, and I want to wipe that smug look off his face. But it's also the truth. That stings more than I'm willing to admit. "Not for long. Pretty soon she'll see you for who you are."

"Oh, I think she already does. And I think she likes what she sees." He winks before strutting away from me.

Blowing out a breath, I slam my hand into a nearby locker. Pain shoots through my fingers, but I welcome it. The thought of that guy touching and kissing Emmy is too much to take. And no amount of punching lockers is going to make me feel better. I'm not sure anything will work right now. Well, anything other than Emmy in my arms. Emmy's mouth on mine. Emmy's hands on my body. Emmy curled against me, skin on skin. Groaning, I bang my head repeatedly against the locker. *Stop it, Chris. Stop it. Stop it.*

"Christian?"

198

I jump at the sound of Emmy's voice.

"Hey." My gaze flickers to the other students passing by throwing me curious glances. Then it shoots to the ground, the lockers, the wall, the floor. Anywhere but her face. I'm afraid she'll see the desire in my eyes, read the thoughts in my mind. Sweat forms on my brow, my face heating up.

"You okay?"

"Uh…yeah." Glancing up, our eyes collide, and my heart stutters in my chest.

She moves closer to me, resting her shoulder against the locker. "You sure?"

I open my mouth to answer when the bell rings out. A kid races down the hallway slamming into Emmy, and she jostles forward. Throwing out my arms I catch her before she topples over. My hands lock around her waist as her body slides against mine. I swallow thickly, my mouth dry, as I lower my gaze to hers. Our faces are so close if I bend forward our lips will touch. And it takes every ounce of willpower I have not to do that. Gripping tighter to her waist, I stare deeply into her eyes as if

199

begging her to give me permission to keep holding her, to touch her, to kiss her. Hell, I wish I didn't need permission. I wish she was mine. I wish I had the right to touch her like this.

But I don't.

She's not mine.

She's his.

Shuddering, I step back and release her.

"Um…thanks." She lowers her gaze to the floor. "I better get to class."

"Yeah, me too." As I watch her walk away, I breathe deeply to slow down the racing of my heart.

EMMY

Something's not right.

Josh has been acting off all day. Actually, he's acting a lot like he used to. Like the Josh before the bonfire party. He's distant, and a little on edge. I keep asking if he's angry with me, but he assures me he isn't. Regardless, he's no fun to be around. This morning he asked if I wanted to hang out this afternoon, catch a movie or something. Since the storm is still raging, baseball practice has been cancelled. And it did sound kind of fun earlier. Normally in the afternoons I just hang in my room doing homework and stuff. However, now that we're at his house, all I want to do is take off.

We're sitting on the couch and Josh is scrolling the movie times on his phone. "There's nothin' good showing."

"That's okay. We don't have to see a movie."

"Really?" He turns to me.

"Yeah." The way his gaze roams my body, I can tell he thinks I'm giving him an invitation to do something else, and that makes my skin crawl. There's no way I can make out with Josh this afternoon. It wouldn't be right. Not when I've spent all day fantasizing about someone else. I haven't been able to stop thinking about the way Christian held me in the school hallway earlier, about how good it felt when his hand slid against my waist. About how much I wished he would kiss me. When Josh's face nears mine, I scramble off the couch. "Um…I really should get going anyway. I have a ton of homework."

Ashley texted me earlier to see if I wanted to hang out this afternoon. I contemplate heading over to her house after this, but I don't know if I'm up for Ashley either. I think I want to go home.

Josh grunts, shaking his head. "Whatever."

Irritation blossoms inside of me. I'm tired of Josh and his attitude. Truth is, I'm tired of the whole relationship. If we can even call it a relationship. At this point I'm only using him as a way to get over Christian, and it's not even accomplishing its goal. I need to call the whole thing off. The sad thing is that when I do, I doubt Josh will even care. Half the time I'm not sure he likes me.

"Josh," I start, but he waves away my words.

That's when I notice his phone buzzing. He brings it up to his ear. "Hey, man. What's up?" He pauses. "No way." Another pause. "That's dope."

I roll my eyes. It's the most enthusiasm I've seen from him all day. With my hand on my hip, I wait while he talks to who I'm assuming is either Chase or Nolan. They're the only people who elicit this much excitement from him. But as the conversation drones on, I get bored. He doesn't even seem to notice I'm still here.

Oh well. Shaking my head, I pick up my purse and stalk to the front door. Once outside, I hurry toward my car, jump inside and head home. As I drive, I decide that the next time I talk to Josh

I'm breaking things off. This entire thing has gone on long enough. Even if I can't have Christian, I don't want to be with Josh. Being alone might scare me, but it can't be worse than being in this kind of relationship.

When I turn onto my street, I spot Ashley's car parked in my driveway. *That's weird.* I know I told her I was hanging out with Josh. I wonder if maybe she forgot. Or maybe she talked to him and he told her I left. I park along the curb and cut the engine. I'm not really in the mood for Ashley, but I guess I have to be now. And that's kind of how it goes when you're her friend. She likes to show up unannounced. It's sort of her thing. Cal says it's because she has no idea how annoying she is, but he doesn't know her like I do. Her home life is pretty sad. I think a lot of her behavior is to mask how lonely and unhappy she is.

With that in mind, I trek up the driveway and unlock the front door. When I step inside, I expect to see Ashley pop out, squeal, and wrap me in one of her perfumed hugs. But instead silence greets me. I do detect the faint smell of her perfume, though, and I follow its trail. As I near my room, I assume she's waiting for me inside. Probably perusing my closet or going through my CD's. My door is closed, so I pop it open. It's empty.

Perplexed, I drop my backpack on the floor.

That's when I hear Ashley giggling, and it's coming from Cal's room. *Great. If she's bothering him I'm never going to hear the end of this.* Groaning, I race toward the sound. When I reach his room, the door is ajar and I press my palm to it, opening it the rest of the way.

Then I inhale sharply, my eyes widening. What the ---

I don't know where to look.

Everywhere my eyes land seems wrong.

Cal's lips…on Ashley's lips.

Ashley's hands….under Cal's shirt.

Cal's fingers…tangled in Ashley's hair.

Their legs…woven together so tightly it takes me a minute to decipher which ones are which.

Gasping, I take several steps backwards

until my tailbone hits the opposite wall. Cal's head swivels in my direction. His face pales, his mouth dropping open. "Emmy!"

I shake my head. *No way. This can't be happening.* He doesn't even like her. He tells me all the time. Unless he only said that to keep me from finding out. How long has this been going on? Heart hammering in my chest, I flee down the hallway and run to my bedroom. Then I slam my door closed with such force that one of the pictures on the wall falls to the ground. It's of Ashley and me, so it seems fitting. I almost fling it across the room. But I don't want to risk cutting my skin on glass.

"Emmy."

I flinch when Cal pounds on my door.

"C'mon. Open up."

I think about how I felt so guilty when I kissed Christian. It's funny how I was worried about Cal's feelings when clearly he's not worried about mine. Then I realize I'm being unfair. I kissed Cal's best friend. He kissed mine. How is that different? Maybe they really like each other. Perhaps

206

they've been fighting their feelings for my sake. Maybe that's the real reason Cal always says he hates her.

One. Two. Three breaths. I open the door.

"Hey." Cal steps inside. "I'm so sorry."

"How long has this been going on?" I ask.

Ashley appears behind him. I expect her to appear ashamed, but instead she looks smug.

"Not very long," Cal says.

"Oh, c'mon, Cal." Ashley runs her fingernails up Cal's arm. "Don't lie to her. We've been messing around off and on ever since you and I started hanging out."

My jaw drops. And neither of them ever told me?

"Grow up, Em," Ashley says in that condescending tone of hers. "You didn't think I hung out here all the time just for you, did you?"

Her words are like a sucker punch to my gut. I feel so betrayed. By my so called best friend and my brother.

"Just go!" I say to both of them. I can't stand to look at either of them. I need space. I need time to process this.

However, only Ashley listens. She spins around and sashays down the hallway. But not before mouthing, "Call me" to my brother. *Is she for real?*

"Em, what can I say? I'm a guy," Cal says after Ashley leaves. "Ash may be annoying, but she's hot. And she was always throwing herself at me."

"So you don't even like her?" This is nothing like what happened between Christian and me. At least not on my end. I feel sick wondering if this was how Christian saw me though. Did he only kiss me because he thought I was throwing myself at him?

"We were just having fun."

It's the last straw. I glare at him. "Go to hell, Cal." I've never spoken to my brother like that, but I've never been this angry before. I feel so betrayed. I feel so angry.

I feel so alone.

CHRISTIAN

Finally there is a break in the rain, so I head to Cal's. I texted him earlier, but he didn't answer. However, he told me he was hanging out at home this afternoon, so I'll catch him there. See if he wants to throw around the ball. I'm sure he's missing it as much as I am. It's muddy outside, but that's not going to stop us. We can take a little dirt.

I don't see Cal's car outside, but I know that he sometimes parks in the garage. Besides, Emmy's car is here, so I figure if he's not home I'll hang with her for a little while. I tell myself it's purely innocent, but my palms moisten at the thought of being alone with her.

Mustering up all my self-control, I head to the front door. I knock several times before Emmy opens it. Tears streak her face, pain ravaging her features. All the air leaves me like a deflated balloon. Seeing her like this breaks me open, tugs at my heart. I've been trying to keep my distance, but all bets are off now. I tug her into my chest, my hands sweeping up her back. "What happened?"

She doesn't answer immediately. Instead, she peers up at me and sniffles.

"Did Josh hurt you?" Anger surges through me. I've imagined pounding Josh's face in for months. Now it seems like I'll get my chance. I pull back, holding her by the shoulders. "I swear if he did --"

"No." The word slices through mine. Pushing away from me, she wipes the tears from her face. I long to be the one to do that for her. What I wouldn't give to touch her skin, to run my fingertips over her flesh, to comfort her. "Not him." She walks away from the door, shivering. "Come inside. It's cold out there."

After firmly closing the front door, I follow her into the family room where she sinks down onto the couch.

"Then what's going on?" I sit next to her.

"Did you know about Ashley and Cal?" She shakes her head. "Who am I kidding? Of course you did. He tells you everything."

Not this. "Are you saying what I think you are?"

She snorts. "My brother is fooling around with my best friend and you're seriously gonna play dumb?" Throwing up her arms, she turns away from me. "Just go. I can't take anymore lies today."

No way am I leaving her like this. It kills me to see her in pain. Reaching out, I circle my hand around her wrist. Gently I pull her toward me. When she gets close enough, I tuck my finger under her chin and turn her head. "I promise you I'm not lying. I knew nothing about this. If I had I would've had a few choice words for Cal."

Her eyes search mine. "Really?"

"Yes. Really." Our gazes connect. "You trust me, right?"

She nods. "Right now, you're about the only person I trust."

"Even more than Josh?" I raise an eyebrow. It's poor timing, but I have to know.

211

"Oh, yeah. Definitely more than him."

My stomach tightens. "Do I need to kick some ass?"

She smiles, causing my heart to stutter in my chest. I love that I make her smile even after all she's been through. "How about we take on one person at a time?" Sadness flickers in her eyes.

"Why do you stay with him?"

She yanks her arm from my grasp. "Why do you even care?"

Her words stun me. "You know I care about you."

"Yeah, like a little sister." She waves away my words flippantly. "I've heard it before."

"It's not like that," I blurt out.

"Then what is it like?" There's a flicker in her eyes that unnerves me.

I want to tell her how I feel, but I don't know if I can. I've kept it inside so long I'm not sure how to say it. A minute passes in silence. The clock on the wall ticks.

Emmy's gaze falls to her lap. "Forget it." Sighing, she stands. Lifting her hand she cradles

212

her forehead. "I can't talk about Josh with you right now. I just lost my best friend and found out my brother betrayed me. I can't handle anything else." Her body shakes in frustration, and I feel like crap.

"I'm sorry," I say gently.

She glances down at me with a look of surprise. Almost like she'd forgotten I was there for a minute. "The sad thing is that Cal doesn't even like Ashley. He said he was just having fun." A bitter laugh escapes through her perfect heart-shaped lips. "I don't know why I'm surprised. This is what you guys do."

My stomach churns. "What *we* do?"

"Yeah." She shrugs. "It's like when you kissed me and it meant nothing to you."

I leap up. "Is that what you think? That our kiss meant nothing to me?"

"Didn't it?" She appears so vulnerable, I can't stand it.

Needing to touch her, I reach out and swipe my fingertips over her cheek. This is the moment I need to turn around and walk away, but there's no way in hell I'm doing that. Frankly, I've let this charade go on long enough. It's time to lay it all on the line. I'm tired of keeping my feelings private. All it's doing is killing me slowly. "Emmy, that kiss meant *everything* to me. I haven't stopped thinking about it…or you…for one minute since that night."

"But what about what you said afterward? I think your exact words were 'this never happened'. Remember?"

"I never should have said that." I graze my thumb over her smooth skin. "I was scared."

"You? Scared?" She smiles. "I don't believe it. Nothing scares you."

"Nothing, except for you."

"Why?"

"Because you make me feel things I've never felt before." I step closer, my hand curving further around her face. "Because I care about you too much to lose you."

"What makes you think you'll lose me?"

"It's what happens. Love doesn't last forever."

"Sometimes it does. Look at my parents."

"True." I nod.

214

"It's not me you're scared of losing, is it? You're scared of losing Cal. You're scared of losing this family."

She knows me so well. "In the days after our kiss that's all I could think about."

"And now?"

"Now it's killing me to stay away from you. Every time I see you I just want to…" I swallow hard.

"You want to what?"

"I want to do this." Unable to contain myself any longer, I bring up my other arm to grip her waist. Then I draw her into my chest, angling my head downward. Lowering my face, our lips almost touch when there's a knock at the door. "Damn it," I growl. Emmy stiffens, holding her breath. There is fear in her eyes. My protective side rears its head. Holding out my arm, I stand. "Stay here. I'll get it."

"If it's Ashley, I don't want to see her."

"I'll get rid of whoever it is, okay?" I catch her eyes and she nods, trust evident. It makes my heart swell. Leaving Emmy in the family room, I take large strides to reach the front door. When I swing it open, my stomach drops. "What are you doing here?"

Josh's eyebrows furrow in a quizzical look. "You the guard dog or what? I came to see my girlfriend." With a look of disgust, he shoves past me.

It's all I can do not grab him by the arm and restrain him. The only reason I hold back is because I'm not sure Emmy can handle it today, but I'm still not letting him anywhere near her. Stepping in front of him, I block his path.

"Emmy's not up for visitors right now."

"Visitors?" Josh cocks his head. "What is this? The damn hospital? I don't know what game you're playing, but you better step aside and let me see my girlfriend."

"I'm not stepping aside," I say firmly. "Not ever again." Glaring at him, I hope he catches my double meaning.

"I know you've got a hard on for my girl, but she wants me. Not you. Got it."

I wonder if he'd say that if he'd seen what

was about to happen.

"Josh?" Emmy's sweet, lyrical voice rings out.

He tosses me an I-told-you-so-look. The fight drains from within me. He may be an ass, but he's right about one thing. She's chosen him. Not me. Blowing out a breath, I step aside and allow him to pass me. But not before seeing the triumphant expression on his face.

"Hey, baby, what's wrong?" He asks.

I can't watch this shit.

"I'm gonna go," I mumble, heading for the door.

"Christian, wait." Emmy hurries after me.

When I reach the door, I swing around. The minute her light eyes meet mine, my heart softens. *Man, she owns me.*

"Don't leave mad."

Her words are like a punch to the gut. I thought she was going to stop at the word "leave". I thought she was asking me to stay. But no, she was asking me not to be mad.

Too. Flippin'. Late. I was mad the minute she

let that idiot into the house.

My gaze flickers over her shoulder to where Josh watches us with a wary expression. Leaning down, I whisper, "Ask him to go, and I won't leave at all. And I sure as hell won't be mad."

Conflict rages like a storm in her eyes.

"You can't have us both, Emmy. I've told you how I feel. If you don't feel the same way, then fine. Own up to it. But if you do, you need to cut the extra baggage," I speak softly, yet harshly. "I want you, but I won't be strung along." Stepping back, I say, "Ball's in your court." Spinning on my heels, I open the front door and step outside without bothering to look back. I don't want to know her reaction. I won't be able to stand it if I see that she isn't watching me; if I see that she's running back to him.

Without meaning to, I slam the door shut.

Hard. Too hard.

The windows shake with the force. Sometimes my emotions get the best of me, and I underestimate my own strength.

"Whoa. What did that door ever do to

you?" Cal swaggers in my direction.

Cal and I have only been in a few fights over the years. Normally we see eye-to-eye. Cal's a good guy. I trust him. And I certainly never thought I'd have to protect Emmy from him. But I guess there's a first time for everything.

"Ashley? Really?" I cross my arms over my chest.

"She told ya, huh?" He looks toward the house.

I nod. My stomach knots when I think about Emmy inside with Josh. A part of me wants to know what they're talking about, but the other part of me is sick just picturing it. "She's pretty upset."

"Yeah, she took it hard. I'm not sure why."

I cock my head to the side in disbelief. "You may be a lot of things, man, but you're not stupid."

"What's that supposed to mean?" His eyebrows knit together.

"C'mon, it's her best friend. Of course she'd be upset." The minute the words leave my mouth I feel like a hypocrite. I'm the last person who should be judging him for this. And really, I'm not. I don't care if he wants to be with Ashley. Well, other than the fact that I can't stand her, and I know he can do better. But my main concern right now is Emmy, and judging by how upset she is, I'm guessing there's a lot more to this story.

He shrugs. "She'll get over it."

I'm surprised by how callous he's being. For someone who has spent the past sixteen years defending his sister, his behavior is baffling. "It doesn't bother you at all that you've hurt Emmy?"

"Dude, you know my sister. She's overdramatic. By tomorrow she'll move on to something else to cry over." He grins. "Besides, it's not like I did anything bad. So, I messed around with Ashley. Who hasn't?"

He has a point. Ashley's been around the block a few times. I can't count how many times she's come on to me. Fortunately, I never took the bait. Then again, desperation is not a turn on for me. I thought Cal felt the same way.

"But if you didn't think it was wrong, why

keep it a secret?"

He shrugs. "I don't know. She's the one who didn't want Emmy to know, so I went along with it. And, honestly, it was kind of a turn on to keep it under wraps."

I shake my head, still trying to process this. A montage of Ashley and Cal bickering floats through my mind. "I thought you hated Ashley." That's the part that bothers me. If he had a thing for Ashley I could understand that. Hell, I've been pining away for his sister behind his back. I get that you can't always chose who you like.

"You know what they say, man. There's a fine line between love and hate. Ash knew how to get me to cross it."

I pause. "Do you actually like her?"

"Nah." He shakes his head. "But she's hot. And a hella good kisser."

"Dude," I start, but Cal cuts me off.

"Don't worry. After my sister threw her royal hissy fit, I broke things off with Ashley. Nothing will happen between us again." He looks at me pointedly. "So, we good?"

"I'm not the one you should be asking." The minute I raise my thumb toward the house, the front door bursts open.

Josh stalks outside, a frown on his face. His expression stops me cold. Dude looks pissed. And his cheek is bright red. *What the hell?*

"Congratulations. Looks like you got what you wanted," Josh snaps at me before storming down the driveway and hopping in his car.

"What was that about?" Cal asks, a perplexed look on his face.

"No idea," I lie. But deep down, my insides are having a freaking party. Did she really end things with him? And did she say it was for me? The longer Cal stares at me, the more I worry he'll figure out what I'm thinking. If Emmy's chosen me, I'll have to tell Cal everything. But I'm not ready yet. Not until I know for sure. "Um…we should go see if she's okay."

"Be my guest. The last time I saw her she told me to go to hell. So I think I'll give her some more time to cool her jets."

Relief floods me, but I keep my face neutral.

"Okay. I'll let you know how it goes."

"Thanks for taking one for the team, bro." Cal chuckles as I head for the front door. "Good luck."

"Thanks," I mumble. *I'll take all the luck I can get.*

EMMY

"What the hell?" Josh barks. That's what it sounds like. Like a dog barking at me. Incessantly. It never stops. All his stupid yapping. "You take off while I'm talking to Chase on the phone without even saying goodbye. Then I send you a million texts, and you never respond. But when I show up here you're with him?"

With a groan, I put my head in my hands. This has gone on long enough. Lifting my head, I face him. "Did you ever think that if I wasn't texting you back that I didn't want to see you?"

Stunned, he recoils.

Yeah, that's right. "Doormat Emmy" has left the building.

He takes a few steps toward me. "What is this about?" His gaze lowers to my dampened cheeks. "Was he telling you lies about me? Because I haven't cheated on you, no matter what anyone else says."

Lame. "I never said anything about you cheating. Why would you assume that's what this is about?"

"Your eyes are all puffy like you've been crying, and Chris is acting like your freakin' guard dog."

"And the only conclusion you can draw is that he told me you were cheating on me? Why would he say that?" I throw him a challenging look. "Are you?"

"C'mon, baby. I didn't come here to fight." He reaches for me, but I move away, noticing he doesn't deny the accusation. But, honestly, it doesn't matter. Whether or not he's cheating is irrelevant. Either way, I don't want to be with him. And at this point I'm too tired to hash this out with him.

"My being upset has nothing to do with you," I say.

"Then we're cool?" Smiling, he grabs my

hand.

I shake him off. "No, we're not."

"But you just said--"

"I said that I'm not upset with you," I interrupt him. "And I'm not. I just don't want to be with you anymore."

"You've gotta be kidding me."

"'Fraid not." *Man, this guy's ego is infuriating.*

"Is this about *him?*"

I know who he's talking about, and I know that it is about him. At least partially. But not completely. "No, this is about me. This is about what I want."

"And you want *him?*" His nose curls upward in disgust. "You're more like his mom than I thought."

"I'll take that as a compliment," I answer smugly. In my opinion it's an honor to be compared to Olivia.

"Don't." His tone is hard. "I didn't mean it that way."

Every word he says builds on the one before, like a stack of bricks. And they are further

226

proof that I'm making the right choice.

"Well, that's the way I took it," I say.

"Because you want to be just like her – a slut who goes after a cradle robber?"

Now he's gone too far. Without contemplating the repercussions, I reach out and slap him across the face. His head reels back, anger darkening his features. But a small sense of satisfaction fills me when a red mark emerges on his skin.

Grabbing his cheek, he glares at me. "He can have you. In fact, I should've given you to him months ago."

"I was never your property, Josh."

He snorts. "You're right. Property is worth something."

His words sting, but I hold my head high. I will not get upset. And I sure as hell won't cry. He doesn't deserve it.

"I hope you and your cradle robber will be very happy together."

Pressing my lips together, I don't bother to respond. There's no use wasting my voice. Once he leaves, I blow out a breath. It's like a weight has been lifted. My chest expands, air clearing out my lungs and flowing freely. Until now I hadn't even realized how caged in I felt with him. How constricted and repressed.

Outside, I hear males talking. Straining, I try to make out what they're saying, but I can't. However, I know one of them is Christian. I'd recognize his voice anywhere. And merely the sound of his voice sends a shudder down my spine. A car door slams and an engine starts. It's probably Josh. At least I hope it is. I want him long gone. When I hear the front door opening, I take deep cleansing breaths while counting the footsteps on the hardwood floors. One. Two. Three. Four. Five. Six.

Christian stands in the doorway. When he spots me, he freezes, shoving his hands into the pockets of his jeans. My heart hammers in my chest and my palms clam up. I feel like my whole life has been leading up to this moment.

"He's gone?"

I nod.

228

"For good?"

I nod again.

"His cheek?"

"Slapped him," I say softly.

Christian chuckles. "Thatta girl."

I giggle. Only Christian can make me smile right now. He's always had the uncanny ability to make everything better. He steps further into the room, his gaze never leaving mine. It's like there's an invisible string tethering our gazes together. When he reaches me, I swallow hard.

"I'm sorry about Josh," I mumble.

He waves away my words with a flick of my wrist. "I can handle that jerk."

"I mean, I'm sorry for ever going out with him." I suck in a breath as if the air is courage and I'm gathering all I can. It's now or never. He spilled his guts to me. Now it's my turn. "He never meant anything to me. No boy ever has." Cheeks warming, I look down at my feet. "Because my heart has always belonged to you."

CHRISTIAN

Words aren't my friends. English is my worst subject. So I don't even try to articulate my feelings. I'm a doer. I show how I feel with my actions. And the last thing I want to do is screw this up by attempting to be someone I'm not. Bridging the gap between us, I take Emmy's face in my hands. Her eyes widen, her lips parting. Last time we kissed it was soft and gentle. Not this time. This time all of my pent up desire rises to the surface. My lips crash into hers with desperation, with need.

Her fingers brush over my shirt as she touches my waist. Something about her reaching for me breaks me open. As I grip her face tighter, our kiss deepening, it's like I've opened up my veins and am bleeding out. It's like I'm giving her every part of me.

Emmy likes to count. She counts stars, steps, breaths. But as her lips move over mine, I'm the one counting. Counting each frantic beat of my heart, knowing that it beats for her and her alone. It always has. And finally, it's getting what it wants. When her chest presses to mine, our heartbeats mingling, I feel like I've come home.

My tongue slides over hers, tasting every inch of her mouth. Her fruity scent spins around me. Massaging my fingers into her hair, the strands coil around my knuckles. Her hands grip my shirt, warmth fanning over my skin. Her lips are hot and moist, her tongue soft. I never want to break away, I never want to stop kissing her. It's like I'm afraid that when we separate the spell will be broken.

But I know this can't last forever. Cal's waiting outside, and her parents could walk in any minute. Reality washes over me. Blinking, I come out of my daze and step back. Our lips disconnect.

Emmy's are red and swollen, lip-gloss trailing her cheek. Her hair is knotted and messy. And man, it is so sexy. The room comes into focus, my chest tightening. A minute ago I was so sure of what I wanted. Everything felt right. More right than it's ever been. But now I'm not so sure. Emmy and I may want each other, but can this really work?

What will Cal think? What will her parents think? What will my mom think?

Oh, crap.

My head spins. I move away from Emmy, feeling dizzy. Betrayal flashes in her eyes.

"You're gonna do it again, aren't you?" She asks, and I can already see the walls flying up between us.

The sadness in her eyes kills me. "No, I'm not."

She shakes her head. "I know you, Christian, and I can see you pulling away." She drops her head into her hands and groans. "I can't believe I fell for it again."

As scared as I am of the repercussions, I can't do this to her. Besides, I want her too badly to walk away again. My fingers close around her wrists, and I pry her arms away from her face. "Emmy, look at me."

Reluctantly, she lifts her head. Our gazes

collide.

"I'm not pulling away. I won't do that to you again. I promise."

She bites her lip, as if contemplating my words.

"Haven't you ever wondered why I can't stand Josh?"

"I know why."

"No, you don't," I answer. "Everyone thinks it's because of my mom, but that's never been the reason. I get why Josh doesn't like her. I would probably feel the same way if Dan was my dad. And, yeah, the guy's kind of an ass on the baseball field, but so is Chase, and I put up with him. I would've found a way to get along with Josh too if he'd never started dating you. When I found out you two were together, I wanted to kick his ass. Like badly. It was completely irrational, but I couldn't stand the thought of him touching you." I slide my fingers down her arms, my fingertips traveling over her smooth skin. "Or kissing you." Leaning forward, I softly press my lips to her temple. "It tore me apart. I wanted it to be me."

"But you never said anything," she says. "I mean, I've had a crush on you for years, and I had no idea."

"You've always been an important part of my life. I guess I didn't want to screw things up."

"Is that what we're doing?"

"I don't know." I curl my hand around her waist, drawing her to me. "But I'm not sure we have a choice anymore. I know I can't back down from this. Staying away from you is killing me."

"Me too," she breathes.

And it's all I need to know. Crushing her body to mine, I press my lips to hers. I don't care who walks in. She's mine, and I'm not letting her go.

EMMY

I wake up with a smile on my face, the details of yesterday afternoon fresh in my mind. What started as a terrible day ended up being one of the best days of my life. With a sigh, I conjure up the memory of Christian's lips on mine, of his hands on my face and in my hair. I didn't think it was possible for a kiss to be better than our last one, but this one was. Mostly because this time Christian didn't push me away.

He drew me closer.

He stayed.

He made promises.

And I believed him. I still do, but I know it's not going to be easy. Not everyone is going to be as excited as I am about this. And in order for us to be together, we're going to have to tell everyone.

235

And by everyone, I mean Cal. He's the one I'm most worried about.

Before Christian left last night, we decided we'd tell Cal together. For now we'll continue to act like nothing is going on. Then when the time is right, we'll share everything with Cal as gently as we can. I'm in no hurry though. The mere thought of it makes my stomach churn. However, it will be worth it to be with Christian all the time. To have him as my boyfriend for real. It's like a dream come true.

When I step out into the hallway in my pajamas, Cal is waiting for me. He glances down at me sheepishly.

"Em, I'm really sorry about Ashley. I never should've messed around with your friend."

Is she my friend? I'm not even sure anymore. Honestly, I'd sort of forgotten about the whole thing with Ashley and Cal. All I've been thinking about is Christian. Even now it's hard to drum up any anger. My insides are all warm and happy.

"It's okay," I tell him.

He appears confused. "That's it?"

"Yep." I smile, ready to let him off the hook. It was the betrayal that upset me. The being lied to. But I understand the chemistry. Now that I think back, there was always sexual tension between them. I'm kind of surprised I didn't pick up on it sooner. Also, I know my brother. He's never had much self-control when it comes to girls. And I can only imagine how many times Ashley threw herself at him. She never admitted it to me, but deep down I always suspected she had a little crush on Cal.

"But you were so mad yesterday. You told me to go to hell."

"Sorry about that." I grimace. "But I'm over it now."

"Girls." He shakes his head, confusion clouding his eyes.

"Boys," I respond sarcastically, shaking my head too.

Cal chuckles. "Just so you know, I broke things off with Ashley. It won't happen again."

"How did she take it?"

He shrugs. "About like you'd think. That

237

chick is way crazier than you."

I laugh. "You can say that again."

"Okay. That chick is way crazier than you."

"Shut up." I punch him in the shoulder.

"So, we're good?" His eyes search mine.

"We're good."

"What about you and Ashley?"

I bite my lip, thinking. Her hurtful words run through my mind. "I don't think I can be friends with her again. Her kissing you is something I could forgive, but I'm not sure I can get past the way she spoke to me afterward."

"Yeah, she was a real witch," he agrees. "I'm really sorry."

I shrug. "That part isn't your fault." Heading into the bathroom, I think about how quickly life can change. Yesterday I thought Ashley was my best friend, but today it's clear to me that she isn't. Perhaps she never was. Turning on the shower, steam curls around my face. I hold my hand under the water, yanking it back quickly as it scorches my skin. After adjusting the temperature, I try again. Satisfied, I peel off my clothes and step inside. Warm water cascades down my back. I reach for the body wash, remembering how Ashley picked it out for me at the mall. As difficult as it will be, I know what I have to do. I have to cut Ashley out of my life.

And the best way to cut her out is to ignore her completely. A small smile plays on my lips at the thought. Nothing bothers Ashley more than being ignored.

****

My plan to ignore Ashley flies out the window the minute I spot her sitting at our lunch table, her hands all over Josh. First my brother, now my ex-boyfriend? Anger crashes over me, covering me like an ocean wave. It's not because I still want him. I broke up with him. But that doesn't make me any less mad. It's not even the point. The point is that I know Ashley's only doing this to piss me off.

Truth is, I've always known Ashley was one of the mean girls. I've witnessed her in action on more than one occasion. But this is the first time

I've been on the receiving end. And while I shouldn't be surprised, it still stings.

I'm sure she expects me to let it go. Be the doormat everyone's gotten used to me being. But letting Josh loose and admitting my feelings for Christian brought out this boldness I didn't know I had. Holding my head high, I stalk over to the table. When I reach Ashley, I place my hands on my hips.

"What's going on?" I ask.

If I expect her to cower or grovel I am sorely mistaken. Instead she wears an amused smile while she touches Josh's head, running her fingers through his hair. Does she think she's making me jealous? Because she's not. I couldn't care less if she's with Josh. She can have him. He can treat her like shit instead of me. Trust me, if she starts dating him she'll be regretting her decision within the week. I know I did.

"Really?" I ask, dumbfounded. "You want *Josh* now?"

"Ladies, ladies." Josh throws up his hands, wearing an amused expression. "No need to fight over me."

"Don't flatter yourself," I snap at him.

He glares at me. "Jealousy isn't attractive on you, Em."

"I'm not jealous." I shake my head. *It's no use.* Talking to Josh is like talking to a wall. Crossing my arms, I turn to Ashley. "Can we talk alone?"

"I have nothing to say to you." Ashley purses her lips.

"Seriously? You said we were friends. Best friends actually. So I think you owe me an explanation for the way you're acting."

"Excuse us for a minute." She presses her lips to Josh's cheek swiftly and then swings her legs off the bench. Then she tucks her arm through mine the same way she's done a million times. Only it doesn't feel like a friendly gesture today. Walking forward, she guides me away from the table. Once we are out of Josh's earshot, she turns to me.

"I thought you didn't have anything to say to me?" I ask, shaking her arm off.

She shrugs. "I could tell you weren't gonna go away unless I talked to you, so I'll say this once. We were never really friends, okay? And now I don't need you, so we're done."

"What?" Her words don't make any sense.

Sighing, she says, "Didn't you think it was weird that I suddenly wanted to be your friend last year after ignoring you for years?"

I guess I did, but I thought it was because we never really talked before then.

"And people think you're the smart one." She laughs. "Look, you were the means to an end. It was nothing personal."

"Means to what end?" I glance back at the table. "If you wanted to be with Josh, why did you push him on me?" Even as I say the words I know that this can't be about Josh. Ashley and I have been friends since last spring, and I've only been with Josh for four months.

"Not Josh. I'm just having a little fun with him right now. No, it was always about Cal."

My head snaps up. "Cal?"

"Yeah, I've had a crush on Cal for years. He's the reason I attended so many damn baseball games. And he's the reason I kept dating other guys on the team." She frowns. "But he never noticed me. Then one day I saw you sitting in the stands all pathetic and alone. At first I felt sorry for you. But then I saw how Cal treated you and it was clear the two of you were close. That's when I realized that you were the answer. If I befriended you, Cal would be forced to notice me. Plus, I'd have access to him anytime I wanted."

My stomach clenches. Bile rises in my throat, and I swallow it down. I knew she was a bitch, but I had no idea it went this far. "You were using me this whole time?" Thinking about the friends I've dropped for Ashley, the lies I've told, the things I've done, makes me want to puke.

She nods as if she's proud of it. "And it was working too, until you found out and ruined the whole thing."

I think of Cal's words this morning. How he broke things off with Ashley for me.

"I figure if I can't have Cal, I'll settle for Josh. He's been coming on to me for months anyway. We've even made out a few times behind your back, and he's not a bad kisser. I could do worse."

My body goes rigid.

Ashley smiles. "Didn't know that, huh? Thought he was so into you? Yeah, right."

Is anyone genuine? As if in answer to my question, I feel Christian's eyes on me. Turning my head, my gaze meets his. He's sitting at the table with Cal, but his attention is focused on me. And by the tense set of his jaw, I can tell he's worried. I force a nod, and brave smile.

Ashley follows my eyes. "Don't get too comfortable."

"What does that mean?"

"I know you think you have some future with Christian, but I know better. You're an easy target, that's all."

Her words stir doubt in my heart, but when I glance at Christian the doubt is replaced by assuredness. She's wrong about him. She's jaded and mean, and she has no idea what she's talking about. Christian's nothing like her. He's genuine and real. She's the fraud. When I look back at Ashley, I grin. "Thank you."

"What?" I almost laugh at her stunned

expression.

"Thank you for finally coming clean about who you really are." My gaze flickers over to Josh. "And thanks for taking Josh off my hands. I think you two are perfect for each other." With a triumphant smile, I spin around and walk out of the cafeteria. It isn't until I'm outside in the quad that I start to crumble. I'm not upset because I still want Ashley in my life. I'm upset that I allowed her to use me like that. I'm upset that I trusted someone who was lying to me all this time.

Mostly I'm mourning who I thought she was.

And it's something I need to grieve, to feel.

Hurrying through the quad, tears slip down my face. A montage of my friendship with Ashley flips through my mind, and I feel like an idiot. How could I have been so stupid? Of course she never wanted to be my friend. Now that I know the truth, the signs are obvious. All the snide remarks and put downs. How she seemed to only want to hang out with me when it benefited her – like when there was a baseball party, or she needed a scapegoat.

She's right. I *am* an easy target.

The few tears have now turned into a freakin' shower. People look up at me curiously as I hurry past. I lower my head and walk faster. I'm almost to the girls' bathroom when I hear Christian calling out my name.

I whirl around. He steps forward, wrapping me tightly in his embrace.

"Hey." He strokes my hair. "What happened in there?"

"It was all a lie," I choke out, pressing my cheek into Christian's chest. His shirt smells like laundry detergent and soap. It smells like him, and it comforts me.

"What was?"

"Our friendship. Ashley and mine. She was using me to get to Cal." I peer up at him. When he looks down at me, I pray that I won't read pity in his eyes. I don't know if I can handle that right now. I know I was stupid, but I don't want him to think I am.

"Too bad she's not a guy," he says shaking his head.

246

"What?" It's not at all the reaction I was expecting.

"You know I can't hit a girl." He smiles, brushing a stray lock of hair from my face. His calloused finger feels good against my cheek.

A small giggle escapes through my lips. "Is violence your answer for everything?"

"Not everything." He steals a kiss on my lips. It's swift. Just a peck. But it makes my heart pick up speed. And it makes me believe that everything will be okay.

"Well, I don't need you to beat up Ashley."

"What about Josh? I can still beat him up, right?"

I laugh. "You'd like that, wouldn't you?"

"A little bit." He grins. "Okay, you got me. I'd like it a lot."

It's amazing how calm and happy he's made me when I was so upset a couple of minutes ago. I rest my head against his chest, his heartbeat thumping under my cheek, and I sigh contentedly. "Thank you."

"I'm always here for you, Emmy," he says.

"I always have been." He tucks his finger under my chin, lifting my head. "Do you remember in middle school when that punk, Jace, was picking on you?"

"Yeah." I nod. "The one that Cal gave the black eye to." I smile at the memory. "He never bothered me again after that."

"It wasn't Cal."

"What?"

"I'm the one who hit him."

My heart stutters in my chest. "Why did you guys say it was Cal?"

"I'd already been in trouble for fighting, so Cal took the fall for it."

"You've always protected me, haven't you?"

He nods. "And I always will."

CHRISTIAN

I'm late for practice.

I wanted to check on Emmy after school. She's still pretty upset, which makes me more than upset. My blood boils as I put on my catcher's gear. I'm so angry my hands shake, my whole body tensing. Seeing Emmy sad tears me apart, and there's no way I'm letting anyone hurt her again. They'll have to go through me first. I meant what I said. I'll never physically hurt a girl, but Ashley is sorely mistaken if she thinks I'll ever let her near Emmy again. Besides, she doesn't deserve her. Not that I ever thought she did. I can still remember how confused I was when they first started hanging out. Even then I didn't trust Ashley, and I was surprised that Emmy did.

Coach Hopkins hollers in my direction, and

I hurriedly grab my catcher's mask. Most of the team is already out on the field. I jog toward them when I'm jabbed from behind. Swinging around, Josh jogs behind me.

"I saw you with Emmy just now," he says.

"So?"

"So how does it feel to be sloppy seconds?"

I stop jogging, and face him. "What did you say?"

"C'mon, you and I both know she's only with you because she can't have me."

I chuckle. Dude's grasping at straws. "She broke up with you, man. Time to face reality."

"Technically, yes, but I haven't wanted that slut for a long time, and she knew it. Hell, she probably knew about all the girls I had on the side too. I mean, one of them was her best friend, after all."

I see red. Coach Hopkins calls our names, but I ignore him. Shit's going down now. I don't even warn him. I don't say a word. It's not like I think it will be a surprise. He has to know it's been a long time coming. Bringing my arm back, I hurl it forward, my fist connecting with his face. His head snaps back, his body reeling backwards. I don't hesitate. In quick succession I hit him again. That's when I hear our teammates yelling. I can see them coming toward us out of the corner of my eye, but I don't turn. I'm focused solely on Josh.

He comes at me, but I block his arm and hit him again. Blood pours from his nose. Tackling him to the ground, I pin him down, and cock my arm to hit him again. He looks pathetic lying in the grass trying to writhe out of my grasp.

"Chris!" Cal's voice rings out. "Stop, man." His hand lands on my arm – the one I'm about to hit Josh with – and he pulls hard. I attempt to yank my arm away from Cal, but he holds on tighter. "Chris, seriously, calm down."

"Break it up, boys!" Coach Hopkins booms.

The sound of Coach's voice takes some of the fight out of me. Exhaling, I stand. Chase and Nolan race over to Josh, helping him up.

"What the hell is going on?" Cal asks.

Josh stands, wiping blood from his face. "Why don't you tell him, Chris?"

251

Shaking my head, I glare. "If I were you, I'd keep my mouth shut."

"You want to know what's going on? Chris is messing around with your sister, Cal. And it's been happening for awhile."

Cal's head swivels, his eyes piercing mine. "Is this true?"

I swallow hard.

"Tell me he's a lying piece of shit, Chris!" Cal's face reddens in frustration.

"Well, he is a lying piece of shit, but--"

"No!" Cal shouts. "No way. This is unbelievable."

"It's not the way it sounds." I rub my throbbing knuckles.

"So it's not true then? You're not messing around with Emmy?"

"No, we're not really messing around. I mean, we kissed, but---"

"You kissed my sister?"

"Okay, gentlemen. This is not a soap opera, and it's definitely not a boxing rink," Coach Hopkins says. "Deal with your girl drama off the field."

Chase and Nolan help Josh off the field while the other players scatter. Cal shakes his head in disgust.

"I expect this crap from Josh. Hell, I'd expect it from any of the guys on the team. But not you."

"Come on, man--" I start, but he stops me.

"I don't want to hear it. I don't want to hear anything from you. I'm outta here." Tearing his hat off, he starts walking off the field.

"What about practice?" Cal has never missed a practice. Ever.

"I'm not practicing today." With his head down, he sprints toward the locker rooms.

My heart sinks as I watch him. It's not how I wanted him to find out. Emmy and I made a pact that we would do it together. That we'd break it to him gently. Emmy asked me earlier if violence is how I solve everything, and it's a valid question. My temper is always getting me in trouble, and it seems like today is no exception.

EMMY

"What the hell is going on with you and Chris?" Cal rushes into the kitchen where I'm sitting at the counter doing my homework. When I first heard a car pull up outside I assumed it was the neighbor. Cal isn't supposed to be home yet.

"Why aren't you at baseball practice?" I set my pen down on top of my notebook.

"Damn it, Em, don't change the subject." He slams his hand down on the counter, and I flinch. My pen slides off the paper and rolls across the counter. Flinging my hand out, I stop it.

"What's all the noise about?" Mom races out of her office, her eyes wild.

"Emmy's been hooking up with Chris," Cal yells.

Kill me now. I sink down in my chair.

255

"Really?" Mom's eyebrows shoot up, her lips curling upward. "Well, this is interesting."

"Mom, this is not one of your romance novels. This is real life," Cal says, grunting in frustration.

"What's real life?" Dad enters the kitchen, a folder under his arm.

Great. Just what I need. More of an audience.

"Emmy and Christian have been messing around." Cal points at me like we're in a courtroom and the judge asked him to point out the perp.

"We're not messing around," I say when Dad turns to me with an incredulous look.

"Really? Cause that's not what I heard," Cal says.

"Who told you?" I ask.

"Does it matter?" Cal's eyes flash.

"It's just that Christian and I were gonna tell you together." I scratch my head, feeling blindsided by this whole thing. And where is Christian? Still at practice? Something about this smells fishy.

"Since when do you and Chris conspire against me?" Darkness flashes in Cal's eyes.

"We're not conspiring against anyone!"

"Okay, everyone calm down," Dad says, using his best teacher voice. Cal and I have always teased him about his tone only working on his students, not on us.

"I can't calm down." Cal exhales, running a hand over his head. Then he looks straight at me. "You two aren't…you know…doing it, are you?"

"No!" I answer vehemently, and I swear I see Dad sigh in relief. "Definitely not. We just kissed. That's it. I promise."

"Did he kiss you or did you kiss him?" Cal leans toward me.

I furrow my brows. "We kissed each other. It was mutual. Why?"

"I just want to make sure he didn't force himself on you or something," Cal says.

"You know Christian would never do that." I'm shocked at his words. He knows Christian better than anyone.

He shrugs. "And I wanted to make sure you didn't force yourself on him."

I reel back, offended. "What? That's crazy."

"C'mon, we all know you've had a crush on him for years," Cal answers matter-of-factly, and Mom and Dad nod in agreement. My stomach sours.

"I guess it's better than her being with that other kid. What's his name? Josh?" Dad says.

"I actually think Christian and Emmy make a cute couple," Mom muses.

"Eww…no. This is not happening." Cal shakes his head, closing his eyes as if he's trying to erase the whole thing.

"Would you rather have her be with someone who doesn't treat her well?" Mom asks, and I'm grateful for her words. At least someone's in my corner.

"Like Josh?" I add, hoping Cal can see reason. He's been wanting Josh out of my life for so long.

"Yeah, well, Josh is the reason I found all this out." Cal pins me with a challenging stare. "Christian beat the crap out of him at practice today, and when I went to break it up Josh told me about you and Chris. Said you'd been messing around for awhile."

My stomach drops. How did Josh know? The minute the thought enters, understanding dawns on me. "Ashley," I mutter under my breath.

"What?" Cal asks.

"Nothing," I say. "Is Christian okay?"

"Of course. There's not a scratch on him." Pride colors his tone. "Josh didn't fare as well though."

I can't help the smile that leaps to my face. Josh definitely got what was coming to him.

"But you and Chris are done," Cal says with finality.

"You can't tell me what to do." I jump up, my gaze darting to Mom and Dad, willing them to step in. Generally they don't involve themselves in disputes between the two of us, but right now I need them to do something.

"Really? You're gonna pull that shit after what happened yesterday?" Cal throws up his arms in exasperation. "When you found out Ashley and I were hooking up you totally lost it."

"You and Ashley?" Mom looks stunned.

"What are we running here? A brothel?" Dad knits his eyebrows together.

"That was completely different, Cal," I say, ignoring Mom and Dad.

"No, it wasn't," he insists. "And I broke it off with Ashley so now you can break it off with Chris. End of discussion." He slices his arm through the air like it's a sword, and then stomps out of the room.

That went well.

****

I wait until I know Christian is home from practice and then I call him. He answers almost immediately. I've been on edge all night. Ever since Cal came racing in here, accusing me and telling me what to do, my nerves have been frayed. I never expected Cal to embrace the idea of Christian and me right away, but I thought he'd be more understanding than he was. After his display this afternoon, I'm not sure he'll ever accept Christian and I being together.

"I heard what happened." Sitting on my bed, I rest my head against the headboard, the phone pressed to my ear.

"I'm sorry about Josh," Christian says. "He started talking shit about you, and I just lost it."

"I figured that's what happened," I say. "And of course I'm not mad. How can I be when you were just defending me?" Truth is, I don't think I would've ever been angry with him for beating up Josh. The guy's a pain in the ass. Besides, I've seen with him Christian. He's always pushing his buttons. At some point he had to know Christian would snap. Christian's temper isn't exactly a secret.

"I know, but if I'd never hit the guy, Cal wouldn't have found out about you and me the way he did."

"Maybe not, but you don't know. Josh might have said something anyway."

"I don't even know how he knew. I mean, he said he saw us together after school, but we were just talking."

"I'm pretty sure he found out from Ashley." Sullenly, I trace the seam on my bedspread with my fingertip. "Man, I'm such an idiot. I never should've trusted her."

"Hey, no more sad talk, okay? You have me. You don't need Ashley."

I smile. She was never a good friend anyway. "You're right. Besides, we have enough to worry about with Cal."

"Has he calmed down at all?" Christian asks.

"No, he's pretty pissed," I say. "Honestly, I'm worried that he'll never accept this."

"Don't worry about Cal. I'll talk to him. He'll come around."

"I hope you're right." Glancing out my window, my gaze floats to the sky, and I find myself silently counting the twinkling stars.

"Eight," Christian says abruptly.

"Huh?"

"I count eight stars out my window. How many do you see?"

Startled, I glance around. "Have you hidden a nanny-cam or something in here?"

Christian's laugh floats through the line. "I

don't need a camera to know what you're doing. I've known you almost my entire life, and you're always counting something. At night you count the stars."

Sighing, I lie back, resting my head on the bed again. My gaze returns out the window. "You think it's weird, don't you?" I never tell people about my compulsive counting. I'm afraid they'll think I'm a freak. And I'm kind of embarrassed that Christian knows about it. The only other person who does is Cal and he teases me at every opportunity.

"Not at all. I get why you do it."

"Because I'm neurotic?" I joke.

"No," Christian says. "If you're neurotic, then I am too."

"Why? Do you count things too?" I thought I knew almost everything about Christian, but this is new.

"Sort of," he says. "You know the grandfather clock we have in our family room?"

"Yeah, the one that goes off every hour." I snort. "I have no idea how that doesn't drive you and your mom nuts."

"Truth is, it would drive me nuts if it didn't go off. Back in fifth grade it stopped working and Mom had to get it repaired. It didn't chime for almost a week, and it drove me mad. I find comfort in that clock," he explains. "Mom got it the same year she told me about my dad. I was seven. She told me about him because he sent me a birthday card, and she let me call him to say thank you. But he never called back."

My stomach knots as I picture little seven-year-old Christian waiting for a return call from his dad. "I'm sorry," I say quietly.

"Story of my life." He chuckles bitterly. "But then Mom got the clock and it chimed every hour on the hour. It never missed a beat. It was something I could count on."

Staring up at the stars, I breathe deeply. "You do get it."

"It's the reason we lugged that clock all the way to Prairie Creek when we moved. Mom wanted to get rid of it, but I begged her to keep it with us."

"I'm sure you didn't have to beg that hard.

Olivia hates to get rid of stuff."

"True." He chuckles.

"But I'm glad you still have it." I stretch out my legs. "And now that I know how much it means to you, I'll try to not get so irritated with it."

"Deal," Christian says. "So, you never answered my question. How many stars have you counted tonight?"

"There aren't many out tonight, actually, but I can see twelve."

"Emmy, I want you to think of me like I'm one of those stars."

"Bright and twinkling?"

"Yeah, well, I am that," Christian teases, and I giggle. "But no, I mean, someone you can count on."

CHRISTIAN

Our home phone rarely rings. Mom and I both have cell phones, so no one calls our land line. I've often asked Mom why she insists on keeping it. She never has a good answer, yet she never disconnects it either. I think it's more of a sentimental thing at this point. Our phone number is the same one her parents had. Maybe subconsciously this is Mom's way of holding on to them.

Therefore, when a piercing ring fills our house late Monday night while I'm doing my homework, alarm bells sound off in my head. I sit still, listening, while Mom answers. Monday is the one day the shop is closed, so she's home tonight.

"This is Olivia," Mom says to the phantom caller, and I set down my pencil. "What?" A pause. "Oh, my god."

I stand, knocking over my English book with the abrupt motion. It lands in the carpet with a loud thud.

"Ok. Thank you," she says to the caller as I walk down the hallway.

After hanging up, she turns around. I cross my arms over my chest. "What happened?"

She hesitates.

Worry strangles me. "Mom?"

"That was the police. The shop was vandalized."

"Not again," I mumble. The floor flies out from beneath me, and I feel like I'm being catapulted back to my childhood. Back to the last time.

Crude words painted in red decorated the front of the shop. Hurtful words. Words meant to inflict pain. Words I didn't fully understand at my young age. But I knew Mom did by the way her eyes widened as she took them in. The front window was shattered, jagged pieces of glass littering the sidewalk.

I tugged on my mom's sleeve, wanting to

know why. Wanting to know who would do this. When she turned to me her eyes shone, her lips trembling. Emotion welled up inside me, bursting out like a dam that had broken apart. I'd never felt hate before that day. Watching Mom cry filled me with a rage I had never felt before.

And it was that day that I learned the truth about why Mom left Prairie Creek in the first place. I learned the truth about my dad; the truth about my existence, and the destruction it caused in my mom's life.

It was Maise who told me. Mom gave her permission though. Maybe because she's the storyteller. But more than likely it was because it was too painful for Mom to relive.

"Do we need to go down to the shop?" I ask Mom now, shaking away the memories of last time. I don't have time to take the stroll down memory lane right now. I have to be strong for Mom. It's what I've always done.

Sometimes it makes me angry. It shouldn't be me. It never should've been. My dad should be the one looking out for my mom. On nights like this the old feelings of anger and abandonment creep on me. He should be the one to help her, to defend her.

But he's not here.

I am.

It's true that I do sometimes forget my role when it comes to her. Not because I don't know she's the parent, but because she leans on me a lot. I've carried her burdens since before I was old enough to even understand them. I've cleaned up her messes. I've held her when she cried.

And I've had to be strong for her even when I don't feel like it.

But no matter what, I'll never let her down. She's been hurt by too many people. There's no way I'm adding myself to that list.

So I puff out my chest, ready to be the man once again.

But she surprises me by saying, "No, it's fine. I know you have a test tomorrow, so why don't you go back to studying? I just need to make a few phone calls."

"Are you sure?" My brows furrow.

"Yeah. I'm not going to the shop right now. I'll let you know if we need to."

"Okay." I'm skeptical, but I nod obediently and head back to my room. After sitting down at my desk, I pick up my pencil and stare at my notebook. However, it's a losing battle. I can't focus. Mom is on the phone again, but she's speaking so softly I can't pick up what she's saying.

As I listen to her desperate tone, I wonder how many times Mom can deal with this shit. And why now? Why would this happen again after all this time?

As I ponder this, it hits me. *Josh.* This has nothing to do with Mom and her past indiscretions. This has everything to do with Emmy and me. This is my fault. When I chose to go for it with Emmy I didn't think about anyone else. I didn't bother to weigh the consequences. I was being selfish, and it was wrong.

Our choice has blown everything up.

Cal's upset. He still won't talk to me. In our entire friendship we've never gone more than a day or so without talking unless we were on vacation, and never because we were in a fight. Years ago we made a pact that we'd never let a girl get between us, so that's never been an issue for us. Of course, I never thought I'd fall for his sister. That's a game changer.

On top of that, Coach is not happy with me. Not since my fight with Josh during practice. Man, I'm just lucky I didn't get suspended or cut from the team. Even the other guys on the team are wary of me right now. And we're all worried about the season. With so much animosity among us, we're all concerned with how well we'll work together on the field. In the past, our team has been much more cohesive.

But this is the last straw.

How can I continue this relationship knowing it's hurting my mom? She's been through so much, and things were finally looking up for her.

A knock on the door startles me. I hear the click of the door as it opens, then the sound of quiet voices talking in rapid succession. One of them is male. *What is going on?* Dropping my pen, it slides off the desk, landing on the floor. Shoving back my chair, I stand up, and in one large stride I'm out of my room. When I round the corner, my mouth drops open.

Mom is standing in the middle of the room being held and comforted by Mr. Easton. He's whispering words of comfort and stroking her hair.

"What's he doing here?" I ask, and Mom leaps away from him as if he's on fire.

"Well…" she peers over at him, biting her lip. "I called him to tell him what's going on."

Mr. Easton nods, shoving his hands in the pocket of his khakis. And seriously, who wears khakis. Who is this guy?

"Why did you call him?" I'm confused.

"It was Josh who vandalized the shop," Mom says.

"I knew it," I mutter. Then I look at Mr. Easton, narrowing my eyes. "But that still doesn't explain what he's doing here." *And why he was holding you.*

"I'm not pressing charges," Mom says.

"What? Why not?" My pulse quickens.

"Don't worry. I'm going to make him pay

for the damages and clean up everything," Mr. Easton says.

"I'm not talking to you!" I speak through gritted teeth. "Mom." My gaze locks on hers.

"There's more going on here than you known about." Her tone falters.

"Josh is going through a lot right now with the divorce and everything," Mr. Easton adds.

"Divorce?" My body goes hot.

"My wife and I split up."

"Mom," I repeat, although it appears to be pointless. Directing my questions to her doesn't seem to deter Mr. Easton from chiming in. "What's going on?"

She moves closer to Mr. Easton, and my insides churn. *Oh, hell no.* This is not happening. "Don't you dare tell me you two are together." I shake my head as if a simple shake of my head can undo this.

"We didn't mean for it to happen," Mom says.

"I don't get it," I snap. "He treated you like crap when we first moved here. His family practically ran you out of town."

"That was a long time ago. He was angry." I can't believe she's defending him.

"Listen," Mr. Easton says. "I know this is confusing. But your mom and I were very much in love. We were high school sweethearts."

"I know all this." I groan. "I know the whole stupid story. Maise told me years ago about how you and Mom were engaged when she went away to college. And how she had an affair with her professor and that's how she got pregnant with me. I also know that when you found out, you broke up with her and spread rumors about her all over town."

"I was young, and I was hurt," Mr. Easton says.

"She had no one. My dad abandoned her, you abandoned her. She was left alone with no one in the world."

"I wasn't alone." Mom gives me a pointed look. "I had you."

I know she means it as a compliment, but it doesn't feel that way. It never has. I'm the reason my mom's life blew up. Rationally I know it was because of her choice, but my existence was the catalyst. If she had never gotten pregnant, she could have chosen whether or not to tell people about my dad. However, once I came into the picture, she had no choice.

"I made a lot of mistakes back then," Mr. Easton continues. "The biggest one was running right into another relationship."

"But you got married, had a family," I point out.

"Yeah, but I also never stopped loving your mom," he says. "It's ultimately why my marriage failed."

"Dan and I have known each other since we were kids. We've loved each other almost our entire lives. Love like that doesn't just go away, no matter how much you try to keep it buried."

"But then why not stay together in the first place?" I look pointedly at Mr. Easton.

"I almost did stay with her," Mr. Easton confesses. "The summer your mom was pregnant with you she came home. I was already with

Heather, but I went to see your mom. Told her I still loved her, but I just wasn't sure I could get past the betrayal. We were trying to work through some issues when Heather found out. And that's when the harassment really started. Heather spread all kinds of rumors about your mom, and since the town already knew about the affair, they believed them. Only your mom thought I was the one spreading the rumors. Honestly, I didn't even know it was Heather spreading them at the time. I didn't find out until years later, and that's when my marriage really began falling apart." He shakes his head. "Anyway, ultimately your mom was so hurt by the way the town treated her that she left. Went back to Sacramento, told me she wanted nothing to do with me or anyone in Prairie Creek." He glances at my mom, an apology in his eyes. "I never should've let you go. I should've fought harder. I guess I was just so hurt, so angry. And it was easier for me to hate you than it was for me to love you. It was a mistake. One I've paid for ever since"

"I know," Mom says softly. Then she turns her gaze toward me. "I understand why Heather and Josh have been so angry, and I'm sorry I didn't explain it sooner. But Dan and I needed to work through our issues alone. We needed to make sure we were ready to commit to each other for good this time."

I feel sick. "I can't listen to this anymore." Anger pulsates through my veins, and there's no running from it. I'm so mad, I'm shaking.

"Chris, don't do anything stupid," she warns. "I heard about practice this week."

A bitter laugh escapes through my lips, and I shake my head. *Is she for real?*

"What are you gonna do?" She presses.

"None of your damn business," I snap. If she's going to keep things from me, then I can do the same. "God, it's bad enough that you kept this from me, but you also lied."

Confusion fills her eyes.

Really? "When I caught you with him at the store, remember? You told me he was just there buying something for his mom."

She sighs. "I'm sorry. I wasn't ready to tell you. I know you'd act like this."

Screw her. Screw him. Screw it all. Storming back down the hallway, I race into my room, snatch up my keys and jacket. Then I tear out of the house. Mom is hollering, begging me to come back, but I ignore her. After slamming the door shut, I hurry down the walkway.

I almost jump in my car, but then think better of it. I'm too angry to drive. A walk is exactly what I need. I need time to myself to clear my head. Besides, my adrenaline is pumping through me at such a rapid rate, I could stand to work off some of the extra energy. Cold air stings my skin, so I shove my sleeves into my jacket and pull it tight around my body. With clipped strides I make my way down the street. Darkness circles me, and I welcome it.

I pass houses, lights glowing from their windows, and I find my thoughts drifting again to my dad. When I was younger I used to fantasize about what it would be like if he was in my life. Would he read to me at night? Would he join Mom and me when we played games? Would he play catch with me in the yard? Would he attend my baseball games?

278

But as I got older, I realized how pointless it was to think about it. Imagining it didn't change things. My dad has never wanted anything to do with me, and no amount of wishful thinking will change that.

I shove my hands into the pockets of my jacket and keep walking. When I set out, I didn't have a destination in mind. However, when I arrive at Mom's shop it seems like the likely place to end up. The word WHORE is painted in bold red letters across the window. I blow out a breath, my stomach clenching.

Josh is such an ass.

Before I found out about Mom and Mr. Easton dating again, I would've assumed this was meant to get at me. However, now I know better. This is a targeted attack on my mom. This is his twisted way of protecting his family. Of honoring his own mom. It doesn't make it any better though. I still want to drive my fist through his face again.

I've never truly understood Josh's hatred toward my mom until tonight though. Now I see the truth. I see the torch Dan has carried for years.

But when I was a kid I didn't know that. Josh never went to school with us, but I ran into him and his mom in the park a couple of times when I was little. I'll never forget the rude way Mrs. Easton behaved toward my mom; the way she glared and whispered.

But it was Josh's words that hurt. The way he taunted me in the playground, calling my mom names. The words stayed with me, as well as the venom behind them. He was only a child, but he had so much anger, so much hatred. And ever since that day I hated him back. However, the only people I ever shared the details of that day with was Emmy and Cal. That's why they've always understood my feelings for Josh.

It's one of the reasons it bothered me so much when Emmy got together with him. But every time I pressed her about it she said it was so long ago it didn't matter now. She argued that we had been children then and we both had changed. Truth is, her words made sense. Only now I see that Josh never did change.

Until tonight I could never figure out why Josh was so mean about my mom. Even once I knew the whole story it didn't make sense. I mean, if it weren't for the affair, Heather and Dan never would've gotten together and Josh never would've been born. Honestly, I've always felt like Josh should be thanking my mom, not mocking her.

But now I get it. Still, it doesn't change what he's done. It doesn't change the way he's hurt my family.

Shaking my head, anger rises in me. I can't believe Mom isn't pressing charges. As if cleaning up this mess is really going to be enough of a punishment. Has Mr. Easton brainwashed her or something? It's crazy.

"Christian?" A familiar voice calls out into the quiet night.

When I whirl around, Tim stands in front of me. I glance over his shoulder to see his car idling near the curb. I'd been so focused on my thoughts, I hadn't heard him pull up.

"What are you doing here?" I ask.

"Your mom called. She's worried about you."

I snort. "She should've thought about that

before she started seeing that jerk again."

Tim's eyes soften around the edges, the lines crinkling. "I know this is tough for you, Chris."

His words chink away at some of the hardness around my heart. Tim has always been there for me. He's the closest thing I have to a dad. Many times over the years, I've wished he was my dad.

"Come on. Let's get outta here." Tim's gaze flickers to the shop, and he frowns.

"I don't wanna go back home yet." The thought of facing my mom right now turns my stomach.

"You can come back to our house. One of us can drive you home when you're ready," Tim says.

I pause, running a hand over my head. Wind whips into my face, and I shiver. At this point I don't have a better offer, and I have no desire to stay out here in the cold any longer, so I nod. "Okay." Ducking my head, I follow Tim to his car.

It's not until I enter the Fishers' house and

spot Cal sitting on the couch wearing an unreadable expression that I realize this may have been a mistake. With everything going on with my mom tonight, I had forgotten about the fight between Cal and me.

"Chris, honey, I'm so sorry." Maise wraps me in a hug, and I stiffen, my skin crawling. Physical touch is not what I want right now. If anything, I want space. "Are you okay?"

"Let the boy breathe," Tim instructs his wife.

She releases me with a huff.

When I glance up, the air leaves me. Emmy stands behind her mom, staring at me with those wide eyes of hers. A minute ago I wanted to be left alone, but now I am desperate to be touched, to be held. But only by one person.

"Em," I breathe out her name like a prayer. Stepping around Maise, my gaze locks on Emmy's. I hold my arms out, desperate to grab onto her. But when I reach her, I stop short, dropping my arms to my sides. *What am I doing?* Cal shake his head and then leaves the room. My shoulders slump. Emmy lowers her head, looking defeated.

Tim coughs, shifting uncomfortably from one foot to the other.

"I'm going to go call your mom and let her know you're okay, Chris." She pats my shoulder, and then she and Tim leave the family room.

Emmy's gaze follows them and then returns to me. She frowns. "It's never gonna work between us, is it?"

"It doesn't look like it," I admit.

She nods, sadness filling her eyes.

"I'm sorry." I have no idea what else to say. "I didn't know we'd be hurting so many people."

She nods. "I get it. I kind of expected this, actually. I mean, Cal's never gonna come around, and you're getting in trouble with your coach. Besides, I heard what's going on with your mom, so I know you've got a lot on your plate right now."

My heart squeezes, reality slamming into me. Is it really over? It hasn't even started yet. But it's probably for the best. I'll never be able to give Emmy what she needs anyway. Everyone knows I'm damaged goods. "I didn't want it to end like

284

this. Hell, I didn't want it to end at all."

"Me either," she says softly.

I snatch both of her hands up, intertwining our fingers. Man, I want to hold onto her forever. "This was never just fun for me. You know that, right?"

Giggling, her eyes meet mine. "You're saying it wasn't fun?"

"No, it was definitely fun, but it meant something to me too."

"I know."

"And I meant what I said. You can always count on me."

She doesn't look convinced. "Do you think we'll really be able to go back to being just friends now?"

"I think it's gonna be hard. Damn hard. But we'll have to. I mean, what's the alternative? Not being in each other's lives? I can't do that. I can't cut you out of my life."

"I can't cut you out either." Her eyes are filled with pain, and I feel like a jackass for beginning something with her that I can't finish.

"Do you regret it?"

"I regret that it didn't work out, but no." She smiles. "I'll never regret kissing you, because it was pretty great."

"Really? Just 'pretty great', huh?" I joke.

She shrugs. "Yeah, you know. It was okay."

"Okay?" I move in closer. "I think I need to upgrade your opinion of my kissing skills." It's stupid. I know that. The minute my lips line up to hers, I know I'm making a mistake. But the thought of never kissing her again is tearing me up inside. Doesn't everyone deserve one last kiss? Well, then this is ours.

And I'm going to make it a good one.

EMMY

His thumb grazes my cheek, and I shiver. Leaning down, his lips hover mine, and my pulse jumpstarts. Licking my lips, I will my heart to slow, but I know it won't. Not when he's this close. Not when he's about to kiss me. And definitely not when I want him so much. When his other hand curves around my neck, I reach out and slide my palms up his chest. My gaze never leaves his, and I see desperation dancing in his irises. I see need, I see desire.

His top lip brushes mine. He exerts the smallest amount of pressure and then draws back. His fingers tangle in my hair, and he gently pulls me forward. This time both his top and bottom lip press down. I memorize the way his lips feel on mine. With my eyes closed, I'm like a blind person reading braille. I block out all other sounds and movements, focusing only on Christian's hands. On his touch. On his kiss.

If this is all I get, I don't want to ever forget it.

Our other kisses were faster, as if we were following the beat to a hip hop song. This one is like a slow dance. Like we are being led by a long, drawn out ballad. He's taking his time, and I'm grateful. It starts off soft, like the kiss of an ocean breeze. His lips are light and airy, fanning over mine. I bunch my fingers in his shirt, holding on tightly. As his tongue licks out trailing my lips, I open my mouth. When his tongue slides over mine, a soft moan sounds at the back of my throat.

He growls in response, deepening the kiss. My head swirls, and I fight to stay upright. I circle my arms around his neck, my fingertips playing with the edges of his hair.

When he releases me, I want to cry out. I want to draw him back.

But I don't. I slip my arms from his shoulders, and I let him go.

CHRISTIAN

When our lips disconnect, I'm not sure what I had hoped to accomplish. If I was hoping it would satisfy me, I was wrong. All it's done it is make me want her even more. And I can tell she feels the same way by her heavily lidded eyes and content expression. Not that I blame her. The two of us together is electric. Kissing Emmy is nothing like kissing other girls. It's nothing like anything I've ever experienced. Before now, the biggest rush in my life is the feeling I get during a game. When the ball hits my glove, it's like a natural high. But this is even better than that. This is like flying in the clouds, soaring above everything. I've never done drugs, but I imagine that being high is a little like this. Like kissing Emmy.

"Well, you definitely upgraded my opinion."

She grins lazily at me. Her hair is mussed, her lips red.

Crap. I have no idea how I'm going to stay away from her.

Footsteps sound from the hallway, and I step away from Emmy. My heart breaks more the further I get from her. In her eyes, I see my pain reflected. Frowning, I don't break eye contact. It's like I physically can't. Almost like by doing so, our connection will be broken forever.

"Wanna go out back and throw the ball around?"

I flinch upon hearing Cal's voice. Shocked, my eyebrows leap up. He wears his ball cap and holds a baseball in his hand.

"If you stay in here, Mom's gonna make you talk about crap. The choice is yours," Cal says.

My gaze slides back to Emmy. She forces a smile, and nods subtly.

"I'm game." I shrug.

"Cool." Cal tosses the ball straight up and then catches it when it falls. "Let's go."

I can feel Emmy's eyes watching me as I

follow Cal out the back door. As hard as I try to ignore her, I can't. It's like my body is in tune to hers. Before stepping outside, I glance at her one last time. Pausing, I drink in her perfect body, her innocent eyes, and her heart-shaped lips that minutes ago were on mine. It takes all my willpower to turn away.

"Ready?" Cal hollers out harshly.

"Yeah." I blink, forcing myself out of my Emmy-induced haze. I close the back door and hurry out onto the lawn.

The ball comes at me hard. Even harder than usual. When I catch it, my fingers buzz from the force. "Shit, Cal." After throwing it back, I shake my hand out.

Cal doesn't apologize. In fact, he doesn't say a word. Just tosses the ball back. We throw in silence for several minutes. The only sound is the ball whizzing through the air, the clapping of our hands when we catch it, and the rustling of the leaves from the wind. But it's therapeutic. It's exactly what I need.

And Cal knows it.

He knows me better than anyone.

Well, mostly anyone.

A light flicks on inside the house to my right. Without even looking I know it's Emmy's room. Her bedroom overlooks the backyard. My body goes rigid, my pulse picking up speed. Without meaning to, I glance over and catch a splash of blond hair. My lips twitch at the corners.

The ball comes at me, and I swing my hand out. But it's too late. I miss it. After it falls into the grass, I bend over and pick it up. "Sorry," I mumble, and throw it back.

It's dark, but the porch light illuminates Cal's face, revealing his pensive expression when he catches the ball. Tucking the ball into his chest, he studies me a minute. Agitated, I wonder why he's not throwing the ball.

Cal's gaze flits to Emmy's window. I follow it and suck in a breath. Emmy is watching us, her bedroom light haloing her head. *Man, she's gorgeous.*

"Crap," Cal mutters under his breath.

My head snaps to him. "What?"

Shaking his head, he tosses the ball on the

292

ground and it rolls away from him, stopping when it hits the trunk of a nearby tree.

"You've got it bad, dude." Cal blows out a breath, pulling his hat further down his forehead.

I know what he's talking about, and there's no reason to deny it. So, instead I nod slowly.

He grunts, pinching the bridge of his nose like he does when frustrated. "Why does it have to be Emmy?"

"I don't know." I shake my head. "But it is."

"I can see that," he says. "You've never looked at a girl the way you're looking at her tonight." Walking over to the back porch, he lowers himself down onto the first step.

I stay where I'm at, unsure of what to say or do.

"Until now I didn't get it," he adds. "I thought she was like every other girl to you."

Ouch. "I was never just messing around with her, Cal. I wouldn't do that to Emmy."

"But you never said anything," Cal points out. "Why didn't you tell me you were into her?"

293

I point at him. "Exhibit A, man."

He snorts, flashing a small smile. "All right, you got me. I've been kind of an ass about this, but can you blame me? She's my sister, man."

"I know, and I do get it. But you have to know I would never just fool around with her. I mean, c'mon, man, it's Emmy. She's like family to me. For me to go after her, you had to know I really liked her. Truth is, I've kind of had a thing for her since last summer. I never planned to act on it, though, because of our friendship. But then she got in a fight with that douchebag at the bonfire party, and I don't know, I just couldn't help myself anymore. I had to kiss her."

"Okay, okay." He throws up his hands. "Eww. I don't need details."

"Sorry." I chuckle. "We've tried to stay away from each other, but it's not working."

"Clearly." He peers over at Emmy's window, but she's gone. "You better not hurt her." He points at me. "See, this is weird. I'm used to threatening other guys. Not you. Not my best friend."

294

"Look on the bright side. You know me. And you trust me."

"Well, I did before you started fooling around with my sister."

I laugh. "Oh, that's how it's gonna be now, huh?"

"Yeah, it is." Cal smiles. "But I won't stand in your way."

"Thanks, man."

"I'm not doing it for you. I'm doing it for my sanity. My sister's driving me nuts with her droopy face and all her whining lately."

"Really? She's been that sad about it, huh?" I raise a brow.

"Oh, man." He grabs his head in his hands. "I can't even complain about her anymore to you. This sucks."

"Yeah, you can."

"No, I can't, because you have this lovey-dovey look on your face."

"Oh, like the one you had when you talked about Melissa?" I razz him.

"At least Melissa isn't your sister."

295

"C'mon, man, it's not that bad. She could still be with Josh."

"Good point." He nods. "Speaking of which, that was pretty crappy what he did to your mom's shop." All the joking is gone. Cal is dead serious.

My stomach knots. "I don't wanna talk about."

"Fair enough." He throws up his arms. "You're not gonna go bash in his face again, are you?"

"Nah, I think I'm good for now."

"Next time, can you give me a little heads up?"

"Sure," I say.

"Cool." Cal stands up. "I've gotta hit the sack. I have two tests tomorrow, and we have practice."

"Yeah, I better head home too." As I walk toward him, it hits me that I'm stranded here. "You think you can give me a ride?"

Without answering, he disappears through the sliding glass doors. I jog to catch up, but when I

296

make it inside, he's nowhere to be seen. Assuming he's grabbing his keys, I lean up against the couch and wait. When he returns, Emmy is by his side.

"I'm tired, so Emmy's gonna drive you home." He throws me a wink. "Be good," he whispers before vanishing around the corner.

EMMY

"What was that about?" I ask when we head outside. First Cal was completely against Christian and me being together, and now he's asking me to drive him home. He's seriously baffling.

Christian shrugs. "Looks like he's coming around."

My stomach flips at his words. "Really?"

"Yeah," he answers softly. I expect Christian to be as excited as I feel, but he appears guarded.

"What's wrong then? Don't you still want to be together?"

He hesitates, and it causes a tornado to kick up inside my stomach.

"Christian?" I prod.

"Yeah," he answers. "Of course I do. I just

298

have a lot on my mind tonight."

Swallowing hard, I nod. I can't even imagine how he's feeling after everything that's happened. Therefore, I need to put aside my own feelings and be understanding. Christian has never been good at coping with family drama. When he feels threatened or hurt, his first instinct is to pull away, to hide behind the invisible walls he builds around himself.

I learned this the hard way when we were kids. It was the first time his mom's shop was vandalized, and my family showed up to help clean up the damage. Christian was angry, that was obvious. He was kicking the sidewalk, wearing a mad expression. I'd seen Cal mad before, but I could always make him smile, sometimes even laugh. And I mistakenly thought I could do the same with Christian. But I had underestimated the level of his anger.

I approached him wearing a smile, throwing out jokes in an effort to break through his tough exterior. But instead of softening the way Cal usually did, he got more upset. He shoved me away, cursing under his breath. When my lips started to quiver, he called me a cry baby and told me to get lost. Told me I didn't understand what he was going through.

And I guess I didn't.

I'd never been through anything like that before. Honestly, I still haven't. Christian's life has always been harder than mine. He's endured more heartache than I could possibly imagine.

That's why I know I have to tread carefully. I have to give him room to breathe, room to be angry and upset. And I need to make sure I don't give him any reason to pull away from me. So I close my mouth, vowing not to talk unless he invites me to. I know it will be tough, but for Christian I'll do just about anything.

When we get into my car, Christian turns to me. "I'm not ready to go home just yet. Do you think we can go somewhere else first?"

Hope sparks at his words, and I nod eagerly. "Sure. Just tell me where."

****

I'm not surprised when we end up at the baseball field. It's the place he's always found solace, and I know he needs that tonight.

"The first time I played baseball was with Cal." We're sitting in the middle of the field, and Christian picks at a blade of grass. "It was right after we moved to Prairie Creek. By then he already had a great arm, so we started playing catch. He's the one who encouraged me to be a catcher. And since we were so close, it made sense."

"I remember," I say. "I was always so jealous that you two had that. We all know how disastrous it was when I tried to play."

"Ah, you weren't that bad," he says. "You just got scared."

"That may be the understatement of the year." I think about how I'd squeal and duck every time the ball came at me.

"You did get beaned pretty badly though."

"And you were so sweet, making sure I had an ice pack to put on it." In most of my childhood memories, Christian's there. And in many of them, he's the one comforting me, making things better.

"I wish I had an ice pack for you now."

"I think we've graduated from ice packs and bandaids," Christian says, a flicker of a sad smile on his face. "Our problems are a little more complicated now."

"Let's uncomplicate it." I scoot forward until our knees brush.

"I don't think that's a real word."

"I'm into math, not reading, remember?"

Christian chuckles. "How could I forget?"

"Besides, I like it. Uncomplicate. I'm so going to start using it in conversation."

"I'm sure it will make your mother proud."

I wrinkle my nose. "You had to mention her, didn't you?"

"Sorry." He nudges me. "Before I rudely interrupted you were going to explain how we could uncomplicate things."

My palms moisten and my heart picks up speed as I move even closer to Christian. Wind whips into my hair, and it flies around my face. I bat it away and tilt my face toward Christian's.

"Whoa, what's going on?" When Christian

swallows, his neck swells.

I touch his face. "I told you. I'm uncomplicating things."

"Oh, yeah?" He cocks an eyebrow.

"Yeah." Curling my hand around his neck, I angle my head until my top lip sweeps his. Warm breath fans over my skin, and I shiver. Pulling back, I take a deep breath. I have to do this right. It needs to be like last time. Like our perfect kiss from earlier tonight. Christian cares about me. I know he does. I feel it in his kiss, in his touch. I see it in his eyes when he looks at me.

But I know Christian. When things start progressing in any relationship, he gets scared and puts on the brakes. I know it has to do with his dad. About the way he's been rejected and abandoned.

That's why I need to remind him of what we have. In my kiss I have to erase his pain, eradicate the events of the night. I have to make him think of nothing else but me.

Pressing down more firmly, my mouth covers his. Darting my tongue out, I thrust it into his mouth. My fingernails rake over his neck as our tongues meld together. As I kiss him more fervently, an ache spreads through my chest. It grows like an infectious disease. The longer his lips are on mine, the more I need to keep them there. The more I need to ensure this will happen again.

I know I love Christian. I think I've loved him since I was a little kid, following him around like I was his shadow. And even if we can never be together, he'll always have a piece of my heart. I can feel it every time we touch, every time we kiss. My heart reacts. It comes alive. And a part of me wonders if it will always be like this with him.

When we separate, Christian drops his forehead to mine. "How are things less complicated now?"

I draw back, searching his eyes. "The way I see it is that nothing feels complicated when we're together. It feels right, don't you think?"

"Yeah, I do, but it's not that simple."

"Isn't it?" I ask.

His eyes cloud over, and I worry that he won't agree. That my kiss wasn't enough.

"I don't know if I can ignore what I feel for

you. Hell, I've done a pretty crappy job of it so far," Christian says, his hand touching my thigh. A shudder runs through my body.

I want to keep him on this line of thinking. Also, I'm curious, so I ask, "When did you first start to feel this way?"

He grins. "Remember last summer when I got back from vacation with my mom, and you, Cal and I went to the lake? You wore that red bikini?"

My cheeks warm. "You liked that, huh?"

"'Like' would not be the right word."

"I bought that the day before you came back. I couldn't wait to wear it in front of you," I confess.

Christian's expression grows serious. "You wore that for me?"

I nod. "Most of what I've done since the day I met you was for you."

"That long, huh?" His face holds an awed expression.

"You have no idea."

Christian lifts his hand, running the pads of his fingers across my jawline and up to my lips. "I don't want to keep my distance anymore."

"Then don't."

Regret passes over his features. "I've got a lot of baggage, Emmy."

"Who doesn't?" I grab his hand.

"Not like mine."

"I'm not just any girl, Christian. I know you. I know everything, and I'm not scared. I'm not running. Not today. Not tomorrow. Not ever." I hold his gaze.

The clouds in his eyes clear a little. Leaning forward, he kisses me hard, stealing my breath.

CHRISTIAN

It's weird being with Emmy at school; walking the halls with her hand tucked in mine, kissing her in the lunch room, showing her off to my friends. Not weird in a bad way though. Weird in a surreal, awesome way. As I open my locker and she leans against the one next to mine, I'm hit with the memory of the day I held her against a row of lockers to keep her from falling. I remember wanting so badly for her to be mine that day.

And now she is.

Taking advantage of the moment, I curve my hand around her waist and yank her to me. Giggling, she falls against my chest. Dipping my head, I steal a kiss on her lips. It's a quick kiss. More of a tease, really, and it leaves me wanting more. But I know I have to back off. I can't maul Emmy in the middle of the school hallway no matter how badly I want to.

After throwing my book in my backpack, I zip it up and fling it over my shoulder. Smiling, I reach out and thread my fingers through Emmy's. Her skin is soft and smooth against mine. We take a few steps down the hallway when Josh comes around the corner, Ashley's hand tucked in his. Emmy stiffens at my side. Instinctively, I push her back a little and step in front of her as if using my body as a shield.

"What's up, Chris." Josh nods his head in greeting as if we're friends.

What a punk. I don't waste my breath with a response.

"Hey, Em." Grinning, Josh peers behind my back.

I move over, so he can't see her. "Step back." Crossing my arms over my chest, I glower down my nose at him.

"Scared I'm gonna steal your girl, huh?" He chuckles. But when he glances over at Ashley, she frowns at him, and he sobers up.

"Not even a little bit," I say honestly. "But

if you know what's good for you, you'll stay away from her."

"Or what?"

"Or I'll add some more bruises to that face of yours."

"Go ahead." He releases Ashley's hand and then steps forward, puffing out his chest.

I want to. Man, I want to punch him so badly my hand twitches. But he's only challenging me because he knows I won't hit him again. I can't. Coach let it go last time, but he made it clear that he won't do it again. If I get in another fight, I'm out. And I can't risk that. Not with the start of the season looming. Still, I can't let him think he has a green light to bother Emmy or my family whenever he wants.

"Mess with Emmy, or go anywhere near my mom or her shop, and I will. To hell with the team or Coach Hopkins." I narrow my eyes. "And next time you won't get off so easy." My eyes land on the bruises I left last practice. "Trust me. They'll be hauling your ass out on a stretcher when I finish with you."

He keeps that stupid smug smile, but his face drains of color, and I know he got the message. Heard it loud and clear. I can tell Ashley does too by the way her eyes widen. When her gaze rests on me, my face hardens. I won't hurt her, but I'm okay with her being scared of me. I don't want her anywhere near Emmy either. They're both poison in my opinion. Ashley cowers, latching on to Josh.

"And just so you know, I'm not the only person you should be scared of," I add, looking pointedly at Josh. "You damage my mom's shop again, and I'll make sure my mom presses charges. Your dad may have talked her out of it this time, but no way will you get so lucky again." I smile, glancing around at the crowd that's gathered in the hallway. "But I heard you did a knock-out job of cleaning up your mess, so kudos for that. Maybe you can add window washer to your list of career goals. It's gotta be a step up from your other skills." Snickers circle us.

Cursing, he shakes off Ashley's arm and storms down the hallway. Whimpering, she scurries after him, her high-heeled boots clacking on the linoleum. I knew that would piss him off. Mom told me how he spent all night cleaning the derogatory word off the window of the shop. Even though I don't believe it was enough of a punishment, I'm still satisfied to know that he clearly hated it so much. Once they're gone, I turn to Emmy, snatching up both her hands.

"You won't fight him again, will you?" Her eyebrows raise.

"Not if he listens to me," I say, wondering where this sudden desire to defend him is coming from. "Why? You don't still care about him, do you?"

"No." She shakes her head vehemently. "Not at all. Trust me. But I do care about you. And I don't want you to jeopardize your place on the team for him. He's not worth it."

****

My stomach bottoms out when she opens the front door. I came straight from practice. I didn't bother going home to shower even though I knew I should

311

have. I've never wanted anyone like I want Emmy. And I've never felt like this before. Never missed a girl after only a few hours. Never thought about a girl nonstop, even while playing ball.

"Hey." Lowering her gaze, she flutters her long lashes, pink rising on her cheeks. The shyness is new. It started after our first kiss.

Truth is, I kind of like it.

I don't answer her. In fact, I don't say a word. Stepping forward, I frame her face with my hands and crash my lips into hers. A surprised gasp sounds at the back of her throat. But then her hands are on my waist, her mouth responding eagerly. I grip her face tighter, my tongue parting the seam of her lips. I practically growl as her tongue slides over mine. She tastes like candy, and her fruity scent spins around me. Her mouth is hot, her lips moist and soft. I feel the warmth of her fingers through my shirt as her hands travel up my spine. Her touch is gentle and tender, graceful. Unlike mine which is manic and desperate. I try to temper it but I can't seem to slow down. I've been fantasizing about this moment all day.

For the first time in weeks, I was on. Not one pitch got by me. And my arm felt better than it had in ages. It was all this pent up desire. All of this need flowing through me. But Emmy isn't a ball. She's not part of the game. She's a girl. She's beautiful and smart.

And mine.

Forcing my heart to slow a little, I soften my hold on her. I draw my mouth back from hers. But only temporarily. Only long enough to catch my breath. I don't plan to stop kissing her any time soon.

"What was that for?" She speaks against my mouth, her breath tickling my lips.

"I missed you."

"I missed you too." This time she's the one who takes initiative. When her mouth clamps over mine, I clutch her so tightly our heartbeats mingle. As our kiss deepens, I hear loud throat clearing, and I flinch. Tearing my lips from Emmy's, I spot Tim standing over her shoulder, watching us with a serious expression.

I release Emmy and swallow hard.

"Um…hi Mr. Fisher."

He flashes me an amused smile. "Since when do you call me Mr. Fisher?"

"Uh…I don't know. I just thought maybe now I should." I have no idea why I'm acting like a bumbling idiot. This is Tim we're talking about. He's been like a dad to me for years. Everything feels different now though.

"Well, you thought wrong," Tim says. "Your relationship with Emmy may have changed, but your place in this family hasn't."

My heart swells. "I appreciate that, sir…uh…" *Damn it, what is wrong with me?* Tim's eyebrows jump up. I've never called him sir before. "I mean, Tim."

Tim shakes his head, letting out a small chuckle. Then he points behind me. "You're letting in the cold air, Chris."

Emmy giggles, and I blow out a breath.

"Sorry." I guess we'd gotten so caught up in each other we never left the doorway. Reaching out, I slam the door closed. When I turn around, Tim is gone. Emmy drops her head to my chest and laughs.

"Well, that was awkward," she says.

"Little bit." I chuckle lightly. "But at least he's taking this well."

"Surprisingly," she says. "What about Olivia? Does she know about us?"

I nod. "Told her last night. She was cool with it, but I knew she would be."

When she peers up at me, a strand of hair falls in her eyes. I swipe it away with my finger. Then I lean down and gently sweep my lips over hers. My earlier desperation has waned. I'm like an addict who got his fix, and now I can take things slower. This time I go easy on her. I kiss her softly. Once. Twice. Three times. I can practically see her counting, and it makes my heart skip a beat. Then I gently slide my tongue over her lips. When she opens her mouth, a gust of wind hits my back.

"Ah, hell no," Cal's voice startles me.

I pull away from Emmy. Her eyes widen.

"I may have said you two could date, but I don't wanna come home to see that shit." He covers his eyes with his hand and hurries past us, racing down the hallway. When he reaches his room, his door slams shut.

Emmy gives me a sheepish look. "Are you regretting this yet?'

"Never," I assure her.

EMMY

Ashley and I haven't spoken since the day she told me the truth about our friendship. A part of me still feels hurt by how everything went down, but mostly I'm angry. And honestly, the more time I spend away from her, the more perspective I have. Therefore, I have no desire to talk to her ever again.

However, I don't get my wish because today Ashley chooses to break her silence. She has the perfect opening because our teacher is busy with Taylor, the new girl who just started today. Ashley sits behind me in class, and when she first leans forward to whisper in my ear I assume it will be about the new girl. When Mr. West introduced Taylor to the class the girl didn't smile. Instead, she scowled at all of us. And the truth is, she kind of scares me with her ripped jeans, black shirt, dyed

317

hair and array of piercings. We don't have many skater girls around here, so I'm not sure how well she'll fit in.

But Ashley doesn't mention Taylor. In perfect Ashley fashion, she goes straight for the jugular. "I saw you with Christian today, and I thought I should offer you some friendly advice," she whispers harshly.

Keeping my back rigid, I don't turn. I know better. Ashley doesn't give friendly advice. Anything out of her mouth is going to be poison, and I'm not interested in hearing it.

Too bad she doesn't get the hint. Instead she whispers, "Don't get too comfortable with Christian. I mean, I'm sure he's making you a ton of promises right now, but you have to know it's not gonna last."

I bite my lip to keep from responding. It's not like I owe her an explanation. We're not friends anymore.

"Christian's always had commitment issues. You and I both know that. But also, this is his senior year. He's going away to college soon. You're just a way to pass the time until then. And it makes sense that he'd chose you. Like I said before, you're an easy target." Her chair creaks as she settles into it. I guess she's finished.

Taylor moves down the aisle finding a seat near mine and lowering into it. A weird scent, almost like incense, wafts under my nose. Mr. West starts writing an equation on the board, but I can't focus on it. Normally this is the class I can lose myself in. Numbers make sense to me. I find comfort in their order. I like how there is only one right answer, unlike English where it's all conjecture and opinions, where creativity reigns supreme.

But today I find no comfort in any of it. The numbers are like a jumbled mess on the board, all running together like an impressionist painting. I know I shouldn't let Ashely's words get to me. She's just being mean. Spewing her poisonous venom. Only I know there's some truth to what she said. Christian *is* going away to college. He and Cal both are. It's why Cal was dating that college girl in the first place. He said it was because he doesn't want to get tied down to some high school girl only to break it off with her when he leaves.

And as much as it pains me to admit it, Ashley's right about me being an easy target for Christian. I practically threw myself at him. And it's no secret that I've had a crush on him for years. As well as I thought I'd hidden it, I realize now that I was actually pretty obvious. Everyone seemed to pick up on it.

Did Christian already know it too? *Probably*.

When Mr. West calls on me, I scramble around trying to give him the correct answer, but I get it wrong. He furrows his bushy brows, clearly confused. And I don't blame him. I never get the wrong answer. When my gaze flickers over to Ashley, she smiles smugly, and I feel sickened. She knows she's rattled me.

One. Two. Three. Four. I pull in deep breaths, but it's no use. My heart still beats out of control, my nerves still frayed. *Nothing is working for me today*.

The minute the bell rings, I bolt out of the class. I have to get away from Ashley and her knowing stare. As I barrel out the door, I run right into Christian. His arms come around me.

"Whoa. Where's the fire?" he says.

"Sorry." I glance behind me. "I just wanted to get to lunch fast, I guess." Man, that makes me sound lame.

His eyebrows knit together. "Hey." He clutches my arm. "You okay?"

"Yeah," I lie. "Fine." I lower my gaze, staring hard at the toe of my boots.

He doesn't look convinced. "Did something happen in class? You normally love math."

I shrug, knowing I have to give him something. "I just got a problem wrong and it rattled me a little."

He smiles, stealing a quick peck on my cheek. "My little perfectionist." Satisfied, he threads his fingers through mine and guides me down the hall. My chest expands with each step, and I feel lighter by the time we reach the cafeteria. But as we sit down at the lunch table, I can't help but shake the feeling of impending doom. I try to imagine what next year will be like when Cal and Christian are gone. It's not like I didn't know they were leaving. But I hadn't thought much about it until Ashley said something.

I've lost my only friend. Cal and Christian are all I have. Once they're gone I'll be alone.

Again.

"Em." Christian's finger tucks under my chin. "Are you sure you're okay?"

"Yeah." I force a smile.

"Cause you seem off."

This is the only part of dating Christian that's going to be tough. I can't mask my feelings around him. He knows me too well. When Josh and I were dating, I could be so furious I was on the verge of tears and he wouldn't notice. Christian notices the slightest change in my behavior. In some ways I find it comforting. In other ways it can be problematic. A part of me wants to tell him what Ashley said, but I know it will make me sound stupid on so many levels. One, because I should've been prepared for Christian to leave for college. He filled out applications at my house, and my family has discussed college plans with Christian for years. And second, because I shouldn't still be letting

Ashley get to me. I mean, how many times am I going to allow that girl to railroad me?

"I'm not," I say simply. Then I reach into my backpack and pull out my lunch. After grabbing my bottled water out, I unscrew the cap and pour liquid down my parched throat. When I glance back up, Christian is watching me, wearing a pensive look.

Ashley saunters past us, her gaze resting on me for a moment. It's a quick glance, but Christian catches it, and his eyes flash.

"You two have math together, right?" he asks, his tone hard.

I stare at the clock on the wall. One. Two. Three seconds.

"Emmy?"

My gaze snaps to his. "Yes."

He can see right through me. "What did she say to you?"

I hesitate.

"I know she said something, so you might as well tell me." He grabs my hand, stroking my flesh with his fingers. I shiver. "C'mon. Spill. Was it about me? About us?"

I nod. He frowns. I don't want to upset him, so I wave my hand in a nonchalant way. "It was nothing really. She was just trying to get under my skin."

"Seems like it worked."

My chest tightens.

"I want to help you, Emmy. But I can't if you keep things from me."

"Okay." I exhale. "She just made some snide comment about how you're just using me until you leave for college."

His hand curls around mine and squeezes tightly. "But you know that's not true, right?"

I want to answer yes, but the word gets lodged in my throat.

"Emmy?" He leans in closer, his eyes piercing mine. "I thought you trusted me?"

"I do," I breathe. "But I trusted Ashley, and I trusted Josh." Moisture fills my eyes, but I blink it back. "They were both using me."

"They never cared about you like I do. You know that," he says firmly.

"Yeah, I know, but it's not just them." I stare deeply into his eyes, needing some of that wisdom right now. Needing him to see me. "They're not the only ones who cast me aside like I mean nothing."

His eyes soften, and he reaches out to touch my face. "Your mom loves you." He pauses. "She just has a different way of showing it."

I snort. "Yeah, you can say that again."

"But I'm not her either." His thumb grazes my cheek. "I have no intention of casting you aside. You mean a lot to me. You always have."

I nod, knowing he's being truthful. No matter what happens next year or the year after that, I know Christian cares about me. At this moment, he wants to be with me. Not in the way that Ashley or Josh did. This is not the same. How could I ever have doubted him? Leaning forward, I seal his words with a kiss.

"Oh, no." Cal groans. "Don't you two ever take a break?" The bench squeaks when he sits down.

As we draw back from each other, we both

chuckle.

"Not if I can help it," Christian jokes.

"Dude, watch it. That's my sister," Cal banters back.

Christian looks at me, touches my shoulder, and then swings his legs around. "I'll be right back."

I freeze. "Where are you going?"

He smiles, but doesn't answer. His gaze lands on where Ashley stands in the middle of a cluster of her friends. They used to be my friends too, but they don't speak to me anymore. Not that I'm surprised since they were always more Ashley's friends than mine. He's reached her before I can stop him, so I sit in stunned silence and watch from the bench.

"What's going on?" Cal asks me, sensing my tension.

I shake my head, trying to hear what's being said.

"You and I need to talk," Christian says, pointing to Ashley.

She smiles. "Wow, it didn't take long for you to realize you needed a real woman, huh?"

326

Her friends giggle, and my stomach sours. Cal shakes his head in disgust and throws me an apologetic look. I know he feels bad about his part in all this, but I don't blame him. I'm the one who brought her into our lives.

"I didn't just realize that," Christian answers deadpan. "I've always known that, and that's why I never went for you no matter how many times you came on to me." He glances at Ashley's friends. "Which was a lot."

Ashley's face pales, and she purses her lips. "What do you want, Christian?"

"I want you to leave Emmy alone."

Her eyes find mine. "Oh, did I upset her today?" She shakes her head. "I was only trying to help."

"Cut the shit, Ashley. We all know you weren't trying to help. Don't pretend you were ever Emmy's friend," he says, stepping closer to her. "You never fooled me. I could always see right through you. Emmy's too good for you, and you knew it. You've been jealous of her from the get-go. That's the real reason you're doing this."

327

"Jealous of her?" Ashley scoffs. "Yeah, right. What would I have to be jealous of?"

"She's everything you're not," Christian says evenly. "But everything you wish you were. She's the real deal, not some fake imitation like you."

Ashley recoils like she's been slapped, and red spots stain her cheeks. I've never heard anyone talk to her like that, and I can tell she hasn't either.

"Just remember that Emmy has me. I won't let anyone hurt her. Do you understand?"

"I don't want anything to do with her." Emmy turns her nose up at Christian.

"Good. Then we shouldn't have a problem." With that, Christian spins around and heads back to me. Ashley is still watching him when he grabs my hand, hoists me off the bench, and kisses me firmly on the lips.

CHRISTIAN

Eighteen.

Finally an adult. Able to make my own choices. To stand on my own two feet. To be a man.

Then how come the main thing I want is acknowledgment from my dad?

I only saw my dad once. It was when I was sixteen. Cal and I drove all the way to the Bay Area where my dad used to work as a professor. He's retired now, but I had his address from the birthday card he sent me that year. It was full of cash, but I handed it directly to my mom the same way I always did. I didn't want his money.

I wanted him.

But that was the one thing he couldn't give me.

He had his own family. A son and daughter who are grown-ups now. They were raised by him. By my dad. They lived in the same house. They saw him every day. They got a lot more than a measly card once a year and cash in the mail. To his credit, he's always taken care of me financially. He sends money to Mom anytime she asks. It was the agreement they made when she told him she was keeping the baby.

Keeping me.

Even then he told her that he wouldn't leave his wife. He wouldn't be my dad in the way that mattered. He wouldn't be a part of my life. Mom agreed to his terms, and I guess I can't fault her for that. She didn't have any other choice. It's not like she could have made him be with her. But sometimes I wonder about the fairness of it. About how I had no choice in this decision. A decision that affected my life so drastically.

The main reason I made the drive to the Bay Area was because I wanted to see what he looked like. Sure, I'd seen pictures, but that was years ago. Also, I wanted to see what his house looked like. So Cal and I skipped school one day and I drove us out to my dad's. On the way he asked if I was going to go up to the door, if I was going to talk to him. I told him I wasn't sure. But when it was merely a fantasy I did entertain the idea. I pictured myself marching up to his house and introducing myself. I imagined him hugging me, pulling me close, calling me his son.

However, when we got there all my courage waned. It was one thing to think about it, and quite another to actually do it. Instead, I parked across the street. Cal and I sat in the car staring up at the house where my dad lived. The house that under different circumstances could have been mine.

It was hours before he came out. He was old, hair white and patchy on his scalp. Using the help of the railing, he made his way down the steps of his porch. I knew he was older than my mom, but I had no idea how much older. I tried to imagine what he looked like when Mom fell for him. It was hard to picture my mom ever going for this old man. But he must have been more attractive back then.

When he reached the bottom of the stairs, he grabbed a nearby hose, turned it on, and watered the flowers in the yard. About five minutes passed before a woman with dark hair stepped outside. She was older too, and I surmised that she was his wife. Her lips moved as if she was speaking to him. He looked up at her and smiled. She grinned back before disappearing inside the house.

Then a car pulled up to the curb, a young adult man stepping out of the vehicle. When he approached the house, my dad set the hose down and greeted the man with a hug. By the looks of the exchange, I took a wild guess that it was his son. He helped my dad up the stairs, and together they went into the house.

My stomach ached, and I wished I'd never come. I wished I'd never had that glimpse of what could have been. Of the life that was stolen from me.

Today the card arrives in the mail like clockwork. I don't bother opening it, but I hand it to Mom so she can deposit the money. I'm not sure what she does with it. I used to think she spent it on herself, but now that I'm older I'm fairly certain she's stuck it all in a bank account somewhere for me. Not that I want it.

"I can't believe my son is an adult," Mom gushes, her eyes shining.

I roll my eyes at her emotional display.

"Just remember that you'll always be my baby." She reaches for me, wrapping her arms around me in a tight hug. I may be an adult, but I don't fight my mom on this. Truth is, I'm grateful for the affection. Hell, I'm grateful one of my parents wants me at all.

There's a knock on the door and Mom releases me. I give her a funny look when she hurries to answer it. The Fishers are coming over this afternoon, but we're not expecting anyone this early. It feels like someone sits on my chest when I spot Mr. Easton standing on our front porch.

"What's he doing here?" I ask.

"Relax," Mom says. "He's only dropping something off."

"Happy birthday, Christian," Mr. Easton says while handing Mom a box.

333

"Thanks," I mumble, eyeing him skeptically.

Mom whispers a goodbye to him, and then closes the door, clutching the box to her chest. "He's really trying, Chris. You could stand to be a little nicer to him."

I shake my head.

"Anyway, I have something for you." She holds the box out like a peace offering.

I lower my gaze to it. "I don't want anything from him."

"It's not from him." She bites her lip. "Well, not technically."

"What does that mean?" I breathe out.

Mom moves around me, sitting on the couch in the living room. She sets the box on the coffee table and lifts the lid. "All of this stuff was my dad's. He and Dan were close, so he gave Dan this box before he died." Mom smiles, a wistful expression passing over her features. "Dan used to love to go through my dad's baseball cards and stuff."

It's one of the first times I've seen my mom smile when mentioning this part of her past. Losing her dad at such a young age was hard for her, and talking about Dan used to be difficult for her too. Seeing a contented smile on her face cuts to my heart. Some of the hardness on my heart chips away. Moving forward, I sit next to her and peer into the box.

"Man, he had a lot of baseball cards, huh?"

She nods. "He loved sports. Baseball especially." She looks at me. "You remind me of him. Especially as you get older."

It's the first time she's compared me to any man other than my biological father. I swallow down the emotion that rises in my throat.

"He would've loved you."

"You never talk about him," I say.

"It was a tough time in my life, Chris. That whole period of time when my dad was sick and dying was too hard to think about, so I buried it. But along with that, I buried memories of the good times too." She smiles, but her lips quiver. "Lately Dan has been reminding me of those good times, and I've found my heart opening up again. I've been remembering things about my dad that I hadn't really let myself remember before." She touches my arm. "And it feels good. Healing, even."

I dip my hand inside the box and snatch out a faded photograph. It's a black and white photo of a teenage boy wearing a baseball uniform. "Is this your dad?"

She nods. "Yep. That's your grandpa."

I stare at the grainy photo, into the eyes that resemble mine, and for the first time I feel like I truly belong somewhere. Like I have a history, a connection to something, to someone other than my mom. And more importantly, to a man.

A man who I'm sure wouldn't have abandoned me.

One who would've been proud of me.

Maybe Mom's right. Maybe he even would've loved me.

EMMY

Chocolate cake is Christian's favorite.

Honestly, he'll eat anything with chocolate. One Halloween he ate through all his chocolate candy before we even finished trick-or-treating, and he got so sick he missed school the next day. That's why Mom and I bake him a chocolate cake every year for his birthday.

That's also why I get so upset today when I trip and fall, dropping his chocolate cake into the grass outside of his house. Dark brown frosting paints the yard, coating the edges of the blades of grass. I'm sprawled out on the ground, my new pale pink dress hiking up my thighs. And I'm sure my body is now covered in dirt and cake frosting. Hoisting myself up to a seated position, I glance down. *Yep, I'm a mess.* But at least I'm not hurt too badly. Just a scrape on my knee and a few on my forearms. Groaning, I wipe frosting and cake crumbs from my arms and off the front of my dress.

Cal chuckles from over my shoulder. "Only Emmy," he says.

I roll my eyes. "Glad you can find enjoyment in this."

"Be nice to your sister," Dad says, but I can hear the amusement in his tone. "You all right, Em?"

I nod, frantically attempting to clean myself up. A car drives by, and I hide my face, hoping it's not someone I know. The chances of that are slim though. This is Prairie Creek, after all.

"Oh, Emmy." Mom sounds as flustered as I feel. Probably because she spent the past hour baking the cake with me. And now all our hard work is splattered across Olivia's front lawn. "I'll go get a towel or something."

As Mom races toward the front door, Dad and Cal at her heels, I reach up and cringe, realizing that the cake is in my hair too. *Great*. I had spent a considerable amount of time trying to look nice for Christian's birthday party. Cal's right. This kind of thing only happens to me.

"Emmy?" My head snaps up at Christian's voice. He's heading toward me, holding a towel.

Great. Why did Mom send out Christian? As if this isn't humiliating enough.

"You okay?" He lets out a light laugh as he hurries down the stairs.

"Stop laughing at me." I pout, staring dejectedly at the ruined cake.

"I'm sorry." He kneels in front of me. "It's just that you look so cute."

My lips tremble a little as I assess the situation.

"Don't cry." Christian looks mortified.

"But I ruined your cake. Your chocolate cake that I made special for your eighteenth birthday."

"It's okay. I don't need cake," he says.

"But you love chocolate cake."

He studies me, his eyes growing serious. "You're right. I do." His face nears mine. "And I

339

like it even better…" his voice trails off. Moving closer to me, I feel warm breath on my cheek. Then his tongue slips out, sweeping over my skin. I shudder. "on you," he finishes.

"Did I have it on my face?" I ask in horror.

"You did." He smiles, licking his lips. "You don't anymore." His gaze lowers, his eyebrows jumping up. "You do have some here though." Dipping his head, his mouth softly nips at my neck, his tongue sliding over the sensitive flesh. A chill runs down my spine as his mouth trails down my neck. A car drives by, but I hardly register it. My whole body heats up like it's on fire. It takes all of my effort to hold myself upright. My arms tremble, my stomach quivers with desire. He smiles when he draws back, and I take a steadying breath. Holding the towel in his hand, he reaches out and wipes cake from my arms. Then he pries my fingers from where they are gripping at the earth. One by one he swipes the towel over my fingers. "Let me get this too." Lifting his hands, he picks some crumbs out of my hair. With every motion, his flesh brushes against mine. I know it shouldn't be sensual, but honestly it's the most intimate experience of my entire life. Holding my breath, I scarcely move. He's so close our faces are almost touching, and I feel each puff of air, each breath as it fans over my skin. Before finishing, he brushes his lips over mine.

My heart beats manically in my chest. "Was there cake on my lips?" I asked, wondering how it got there.

"No. That was just because I wanted to." He smiles. "But I gotta be honest. That's the best chocolate cake I've ever had." He winks. "You better watch out, because next year I might trip you."

A giggle bursts from my throat. "You better not."

After standing, he extends his hand. I glance at the cake on the ground.

"Don't worry about it," he says as if reading my mind. "The neighborhood dogs will get to it."

Taking his hand, I allow him to help me up. "I'm sorry."

Once I'm standing, he hooks an arm around my waist and tugs me forward. Our chests bump, and then he wraps both arms around my middle. "I don't need the cake. I've got everything I want right here."

****

Christian may have been okay with not having cake, but no one else was. And since I ruined the first one, my mom sent me to the store to get a replacement. The cake from the store can never compare to the one I made, but I figure it will have to do.

When I return back to the house, I take deliberate steps up the walkway. For added insurance, I grip the railing as I make my way up the front porch steps. Clutching tightly to the edges of the cake box, I press open the front door and step inside. Olivia's house smells like pizza, Christian's favorite food. I figure by the time I reach the kitchen Christian will be hunched over the counter wolfing down a piece, cheese dribbling from his chin.

Growing up, Friday nights at our house

were movie and pizza nights. And Christian was present for most of them. He and Cal can put away more pizza than any two people I've ever met. It makes me sick simply watching them.

Wearing a triumphant smile, I round the corner. "I made it! And the cake is still intact."

I'm expecting a collective round of thank yous, but no one says a thing. My gaze sweeps the room, and my stomach tumbles to the floor. Olivia's bottom lip quivers. Mom puts a hand on her shoulder. Dad scratches the back of his neck nervously, and Cal clears his throat. I lower the cake onto the counter.

"Where's Christian?" When no one responds dread sinks into my gut. "What's going on?"

Cal snatches something off the counter and takes a step forward. He holds it out to me. I narrow my eyes, staring at the blue birthday card, a candle drawn on the front. "What's that?"

"It's the birthday card from his dad," Cal responds.

Olivia sniffs, running a hand under her

nose. I don't get it. Christian's dad sends him a card every year, and I know it's hard for him, but he deals with it.

"Just look." Cal thrusts the card into my hand.

I close my fingers around it. My hand shakes violently. When my gaze connects to the words on the card, disbelief fills me. I feel dizzy, lightheaded. Reaching out with my free hand, I grip the edge of the counter. This can't be happening.

"Where did he go?" I ask, my voice wobbly.

Cal shakes his head, worry etching his features. "Don't know."

"You just let him leave?" My gaze darts around the room. "He must be devastated."

"Honey," Dad speaks gently to me. "He took off. We couldn't stop him."

"He probably just needs some space. Some time to cool off," Cal says.

But I can't do that. I can't leave him alone right now. Not when he needs me the most. Flinging the card on the counter, I pivot on my heels.

"Where are you going?" Mom calls.

"To find Christian."

When I reach the door, Cal catches up to me. "Do you think this is a good idea?"

"I can't believe you didn't try to stop him, Cal. I thought he was your best friend."

"He is." Cal's eyes flash. "That's why I didn't stop him."

"He needs us."

"I know Chris. If you push him when he's hurting, he's gonna push back." He clamps a hand down on my shoulder. "Are you prepared for that?"

I'm not sure if I am, but there's no way I can sit idly by when I know that Christian is hurting. He's protected me so much. He's held me when I was sad. He's wiped my tears and helped me when I needed it. Now it's my turn to do the same for him.

CHRISTIAN

Christian,

I regret to your inform you that your father passed away last month. In his will, he asked that I send you one final card wishing you a happy birthday. Also, he wanted me to inform you that he set up a bank account in your name and deposited a substantial amount of money in it. It should be enough to put you through college. Our attorney's card is enclosed. Give him a call, and he will give you all the details.

Happy birthday.

Sincerely,

Bridgett Thomas

Bridgett Thomas. My dad's wife. The woman he chose over my mom. The woman he chose over me. Thinking of her last name, I'm grateful Mom decided to give me hers. There were times when I wished I had my dad's. Mainly when we first moved to Prairie Creek, since everyone knew who's child I was the minute they heard my last name. But today I'm glad I have my mom's. It's fitting since she raised me. Not him. He's a stranger.

And now he's dead.

Left me with nothing more than a birthday card and some money. Not that I should be surprised. It was all he gave me when he was alive too. Apparently it's all I'm ever going to get. Worthless money and worthless cards. A few sentences scrawled on paper. And the last one isn't even from him. He could take the time to write out a will, but he never penned a letter for me. Not a final goodbye or some words of fatherly knowledge or advice. Nothing.

It seems unfathomable that I'll never have anything from my father – my own flesh and blood – other than money and store bought birthday cards. *Wow, what a legacy.*

Livid, I kick at the grass with the toe of my shoe. Didn't he get it? Didn't he know? I never wanted his money. It never meant anything to me.

And it means even less now.

How dare he leave this earth without ever speaking to me. Without ever giving me the chance to tell him how I felt. To tell him what a worthless piece of shit he was. To tell him about everything he missed. To throw my successes in his face. To prove to him that I never needed him in the first place.

Groaning, I move over to the bleachers and kick one of them as hard as I can. Pain shoots through my toe, and I hiss. *Damn it.* I better not have broken it. The last thing I need is to hurt myself over that loser. He doesn't deserve it. In fact, he doesn't deserve any of it.

I should be at home celebrating my birthday with my family and friends. Instead, I'm at the baseball field throwing a fit like a baby. Exhausted and beat down, I climb up the bleachers. At the top, I sit. The bleacher moans beneath my weight. From up here I can see the whole field – the green grass, the shimmering sand, the dugout, batter's box, home plate. This place knows me better than my own father. It's seen me through season after season. Through crushes, breakups, conflicts, makeups, losses, and wins. It's seen me at my best and at my worst.

And it's where I feel most like me.

Resting my head against the railing, I close my eyes. Wind whisks over my face, carrying with it the scent of damp earth. It's cold, but I don't mind it. The image of my dad watering his plants that day I watched him from my car fills my mind. I think of the man he embraced in his yard; the one I assumed was his son. I wonder if he stood by his dad's side when he died. Did he hold his hand, whisper reassuring words in his ear? More importantly, did he know about me – his brother?

Apparently, Bridgette did. Or at least she does now.

If she knew before he died, why didn't she contact me? Why wasn't I given the opportunity to say goodbye? To say anything?

Shaking my head, I curse myself for going in circles. This line of thinking isn't getting me anywhere. It doesn't matter anyway. He's gone. It's time to let him go. And it's not like that should be hard, since I never had him to begin with.

Thinking of the card sitting on the counter at home, my heart hardens further. I'll take his crummy money, and I'll use it for college. But I'm doing it for Mom, and only her. She's the one who matters.

He doesn't. He never did. And he never will.

Bitter tears sting my eyes, and I blink them back furiously. No way am I crying over that bastard. *Never.* Sniffing, I swipe under my nose with my hand. When the bleachers creak, my head snaps up.

"Christian?" Emmy's voice startles me.

I freeze, spotting her climbing towards me. "What are you doing here?" The words come out harsher than I intended, but I don't apologize. I don't take them back.

"Wanted to make sure you were okay." She continues climbing.

My chest tightens. "I'm fine. Just want to be alone."

She stops, her eyebrows knitting together. I pray that she'll take the hint. But she doesn't. She starts climbing again. *I should've known.*

"I don't want wanna hurt your feelings, Emmy," I plead with her.

"Then don't."

"If you don't leave, I can't make any promises." I turn my head away from her. "Please just go."

"But I want to help you," she says softly, her voice coming closer.

Annoyance flares. "Damn it, why are you doing this?"

"Doing what?" She's close now. Too close.

"Pushing me," I say.

"I'm not pushing you. You don't have to say anything. I just want to be here with you."

Desperation blossoms in my chest, and I fight to breathe. "I can't do this right now." This is why I don't do relationships. It's why I stick to hanging with Cal and the guys. Girls don't know when to back off. Cal gives me space when I need it. Clearly, Emmy doesn't. She plops down beside me, her thigh brushing mine. I scoot away.

"I'm not leaving you like this," she says firmly.

And I might think it was sweet, sexy even, if I weren't so pissed. If I didn't feel so claustrophobic, so boxed in.

"Fine." I stand, sucking in a breath. "Then I'll leave."

"Why are you being like this?" She stands too, facing me. Frowning, her eyes are steely. She places a hand on her hip.

"Because this is who I am. I'm broken, damaged, wrecked. I tried to warn you. I tried to keep you away."

She sighs. "You're upset. It's understandable. But this isn't you."

"Yes, it is. I'm the loose cannon. The boy with the bad temper whose dad doesn't want him. It's who I've always been."

Emmy's eyes scan my face. "That's not true." She reaches for me, her hand touching my arm. It's more than I can take. I can't handle pity or comfort right now. It'll tear me apart, break me open. My insides will be laid bare, scattered all over this field. And there's no way I'm letting that happen.

"Don't." I shake her hand off, and her eyes widen. "I can't be with you right now." I can tell she's not buying it. I can see that she's going to keep trying, and I can't have that.

When I first realized I was attracted to Emmy, I kept my distance and told myself it was because of Cal. That it was because of our family. That it was because I didn't want to mess with what I had. But deep down, it must have been because I knew it would end like this. I must have known I was too damaged to ever really love her. I have this hole inside of me that my dad's love should have filled. But it's always been empty, and over the years it's spread; become larger and larger. His death seems to have widened it to astronomical proportions. And now I'm certain I can never be that guy for Emmy. The kind of guy that will love her like she deserves. As much as it kills me, I know I have to put the final nail in the coffin. "Truth is, I'm not sure if I ever can be."

"What?" She reels back, hurt splashed across her features. It's what I wanted, but it's harder than I thought. Still, I have to keep going. I have to be strong.

"I thought I could be a normal guy. The kind of guy who falls in love. The kind of guy who can let someone in. You made me believe that could be possible, and I wanted to be that guy for you. But today I realized that's not me. I'm not that guy, and I never will be."

"I don't understand. What about back at the house. With the cake….on the lawn." She's grasping at memories. I can see the wheels spinning as she's trying to pluck them out, to bring them back to life. But it's no use. The guy I was an hour ago is gone.

Or maybe he was never here at all.

Either way, I feel numb, empty. I want to give Emmy something, but I can't. I'm hollow inside like a pumpkin after being cut open, my insides scraped out. There's nothing inside. Nothing to give. Nothing to share. She deserves so much more than that.

"I'm sorry." It's all I can formulate. Then, shaking my head, I bound down the bleachers. I take them two at a time so I can get to the bottom faster. Emmy calls my name, but I ignore her.

There's nothing left to say.

EMMY

I never should have pushed Christian. I should have listened to Cal. Then maybe Christian wouldn't be ignoring me now. It's been almost a week since we spoke. Even when I pass him in the halls at school, he refuses to make eye contact. He turns his head or stares down at his shoes. Sometimes I think about stepping in his path, of forcing him to acknowledge me. But then I remember how cold he was toward me at the baseball field, and it stops me. It was hard enough to have him treat me like that in private. It would be downright unbearable in front of a bunch of high school students. It was just like when we were kids and I tried to comfort him after the shop was vandalized. But this time I'm not a child, and he hurt a lot more than my pride. He broke my heart. I know Ashley's noticed I'm not with Christian anymore. I've seen her knowing glances, her triumphant smiles. And it makes me sick.

I trusted Christian. I believed him when he told me he wasn't going to hurt me. Ashley knew better. She tried to warn me. And it makes me feel stupid.

At times I've felt so desperate I've contemplated asking Cal to talk to Christian on my behalf, but I can't do that. I don't want to get in the middle of their friendship. I don't want to cause a rift. No matter how angry I am with Christian, I know he's hurting right now. He needs Cal, even if he won't admit it. That's why I've kept my brave face on around Cal. In fact, I didn't even tell him what happened at the baseball field. All I said was that I'd decided to give Christian space to process his dad's death.

It isn't exactly a lie.

It isn't exactly the truth either.

However, it's what I need Cal to believe. And I think he did at first. Now I'm not so sure. The last couple of days he's been watching me more closely, asking pointed questions. As hard as I try to keep up this ruse, I know he'll see through me at some point. Like a spool of yarn, I'm starting to unravel a little more every day. I envision my insides trailing me everywhere I go. My nerves are frayed, my emotions lingering right at the surface.

When I get home from school Friday, I find Olivia sitting at the kitchen table drinking a cup of tea with Mom. They are deep in conversation, their heads bent close together. Everything about them is opposite in looks. Where Mom has light hair, Olivia's is dark. Mom's skin is pale, Olivia's is tanned. Olivia dresses very eclectic, while Mom favors yoga pants and t-shirts. However, when they are seated like this they mirror each other. As their mouths move, words spilling across the table, I can see the similarities. Not so much in how they look, but in who they are.

The minute I enter the room the spell is broken. Their heads bounce up and they greet me. Then Mom waves me over, inviting me to join them. Normally I would jump at the chance. When I was a little girl, I loved to watch them sit and drink tea together. They would gab about life, holding pretty mugs in their hands. I'd watch as steam rose from the cups, and I'd dream of one day joining them. When I got older, they'd allow me to sit with them from time to time, and I loved it. But today I don't think I can. I don't know if I can sit across from Olivia without giving away how I feel; without spilling my guts about Christian. So I shake my head, declining the invitation. However, Mom insists, not taking no for an answer.

Olivia gets up from the table and envelopes me in a hug. And that's when I lose it. Sobs rack my body. Tears fill my eyes. I'm grasping at the edge of the yarn, desperately trying to reign myself in, but it slips through my fingers. It's no use. I'm coming undone.

"Oh, honey." Olivia strokes my hair. "It's going to be okay."

I peer up at her, blinking through the haze of tears. Does she know?

When our eyes lock, I know that she does. Brushing a damp strand of hair from my face, she says, "Trust me, Chris will come around."

"He will?" I ask, and it terrifies me how much I need to believe her words.

She nods.

"How do you know?"

"Because I know him." She smiles. "I know him better than anyone."

That's true. She does. If I can trust anyone when it comes to Christian, it's the woman who raised him.

She draws back from me, and squeezes my hand. "C'mon. Let's sit down and have a cup of tea."

Mom already has a steaming cup on the table for me. I sit in the empty chair in front of it. When my hand closes around it, warmth seeps into my palm. Lifting the mug to my lips, I take a tentative sip. It's hot, but not too hot, and it feels good as it coats my tongue. Tea has always had a calming effect on me.

"How is he?" I ask Olivia.

"He's struggling," she answers honestly. "He misses you."

"He said that?" Hope stirs in my heart.

Olivia shakes her head. "No, but I can tell."

I frown.

"Oh, you know how guys are," Mom says as if she's an expert. "They don't talk about their feelings, but we can read them. Isn't that right, Liv?"

Olivia chuckles. "Yes, we can. And there's no boy on earth I can read better than Chris."

"He told me to leave him alone. Said he couldn't be with me anymore," I confess. "And now he won't talk to me."

I don't realize that Cal is home until I hear the sharp intake of breath from over my shoulder. When I turn around, Cal's eyes are narrowed, his mouth pressed together in a tight line.

"You told me you decided to give him space. You never said he told you to leave him alone," Cal says angrily.

Olivia stiffens.

Mom sits up straighter. "Cal, you know better than to eavesdrop on girl talk."

"Emmy," Cal presses. When my gaze meets his, he shakes his head. "Damn it, have you been crying?"

"Cal." I push away from the table, and stand. "I'm fine." When he flashes me a look of disbelief, I say, "Err...I'll be fine."

Cal curses under his breath, slamming his palm on the counter. "I can't believe him. He promised me he wouldn't hurt you."

"Cal, stay out of it," Mom says from where she sits at the table. "This is between Chris and Emmy. They don't need you meddling. You don't want to stand in the way of love, do you?"

By the look on Cal's face, I'd say she lost him with the last statement. But that's Mom. She always goes too far.

"Can you keep your flowery sentiments in your books, please?" Cal says. "Chris and Emmy aren't one of the couples you made up, and I'm not letting him get away with this." Angrily, he storms out of the room.

I glance at his back helplessly.

"Just let him go," Mom says. "Let him cool down."

My instinct is to go after him, but I decide

to listen to Mom. I decide to give him his space. I do for Cal what I should have done for Christian. But I pray that it's the right decision.

I pray that Cal doesn't make everything worse.

CHRISTIAN

We lost the scrimmage tonight, and it's Cal's fault. He missed all my signals and his throws were wild. I've never seen him play like that, and it's making me worry about the start of the season in a couple of weeks.

After the scrimmage I pass him, and his shoulder slams into mine. *Okay, that's it.*

"What the hell is wrong with you?" I snap.

"With me?" His eyes widen incredulously. "What's wrong with you?" Pressing his palms into my chest, he shoves me backward. The other players glance over, and I can feel the tension rising. I cock my head to the side, confused, when he shoves me again. *Oh, hell no.* "You said I could trust you. Said you wouldn't hurt her." Another push.

Ah, this is about Emmy. I should've known.

Softening, I take a deep breath and put out my hands to stop him from shoving me again. "I'm sorry, man. I never should've made that promise."

"Wow." He nods, an angry smile painting his face. "Never pegged you as a coward."

Coward? Anger surfaces. "What did you say to me?" I step forward, fisting my hands at my sides. Some of the guys move closer, whispering to one another. They're expecting a fight.

"Go ahead." He lifts his chin. "Hit me. It won't prove anything. Won't make you any less of a coward."

"I'm warning you, Cal," I growl, my arms twitching, my veins pulsating beneath my flesh.

"Go ahead. Do it"

He's egging me on. He wants me to hit him, and he knows how to push my buttons. I blow out a breath. No way. I can't do it. Not to Cal. I take a step back. "I'm not hitting you."

"Why not?"

"Cause you're my best friend, man."

"So what? So, you'll burn another bridge," he says. "Then you'll be alone. Isn't that what you want?"

His words hurt worse than a punch.

Cal laughs bitterly, shaking his head. "You know what's funny? You hate your old man so much, but you're just like him. Running away the same way he did."

Now he's gone too far. I plant my hands squarely in his chest and shove him back. He flies backward, but stays on his feet. Wearing a smile, his eyes never leave mine. Unnerved, I avert my gaze. Hurrying away from him, I grab my stuff. I'm not sticking around here for one more minute.

Adrenaline pumping, body shaking, I walk swiftly across the darkened field toward the parking lot. I almost reach it when I see Emmy standing at the edge of the grass staring up at the stars. Spinning around, I plan to run in the other direction, but then Cal's words fill my mind.

You're just like him. Running away the same way he did.

She looks so lost standing there all alone, and I can't leave her. Not now. Not tonight. Gathering all my courage, I head in her direction.

366

When I reach her, she peers over her shoulder. Her face is unreadable, but she doesn't appear too shocked to see me. It's almost like she had been waiting for me. Maybe she was.

"Two hundred twenty-five," she says.

"What?"

"That's how many stars I've counted since you last spoke to me."

Ouch. "Emmy, I--"

"You said you were my star." She whirls around to face me, her eyes flashing with pain and anger. "You said I could count on you." Her index finger flies out, jabbing me in the chest right above my heart, emphasizing every syllable. It stings a little, but I take it. It's the least I can do. "But you lied." She draws her arm back. "And you know what's sad? You knew how much saying that would mean to me, because you know me."

"I do know you. You're right." My shoulders slump, my head hanging low. I feel defeated. "But you know me too," I point out. She knew all about my scars before we started dating.

"I thought I did, but apparently I never

knew at all."

My heart falters. "That's not true."

"Yeah, it is." Her eyes shine in the moonlight. "Cause the Christian I know would never hurt me like this."

"I never meant to hurt you." I reach my arms out, but then drop them. No matter how much I want to touch her, that would be selfish right now.

"And yet you did."

My heart crashes to the ground, bursting into flames. I imagine smoke pluming around us. "I wanted this to work. I really did."

"That's such a cop-out." She shakes her head.

It angers me. It's so easy to point fingers, to shift blame, but she has no idea what I've been through. How hard all of this has been for me. "Do you have any idea what it feels like to be rejected by your dad? Not one time or two times." My voice is rising, the strap from my bag slipping from my shoulder. I shove it back up and continue. "No. He rejected me my entire life, and now he's gone. I'll never have the chance to talk to him, to tell him how I feel. Do you get that?"

She nods subtly, her lower lip trembling slightly. And I feel like a jerk. I shouldn't have been so harsh with her, but I need to make her understand.

Biting down on her lip, she composes herself. "I do get it. I know your dad hurt you. I know he never chose you, but someone else did. Olivia gave up everything for you. She was disowned, ostracized, ridiculed. All because she chose you, Christian."

Emotion rises in me at her words, and I swallow it down, not wanting to feel it.

"And she's not the only one. Cal chose you. My parents chose you." Her eyes crash into mine. "And I chose you." She pauses, holding my gaze steady. "I still do."

I want her. Lord knows I want her. More than anything. But I can't hurt her anymore. I can't pull her back only to push her away again. How do I make her see that I'm doing this because I care about her?

I put my hand over my heart. "There's something missing in here now. It's like a part of me died with him, and I don't know how to do this anymore."

One eyebrow cocks. "Do what?"

"This." I point between us. "I don't know how to open myself up to you."

When she smiles, I'm surprised. Then she steps toward me, placing a hand on my waist, and I'm downright stunned. *What the hell is she up to?* I should draw back, but I stay put, rooted in place. "Don't you remember what I said about uncomplicating things?"

"Oh, we're back to that, are we?" I can't help it. I laugh. And it feels good. Damn good.

She nods. Then before I can stop her, she kisses me. And heaven help me, I respond to it. I more than respond to it. I kiss her back with vigor. Flinging my bat bag on the ground, I sweep my hands up, funneling my fingers through her hair. Gripping her face between my palms, my mouth presses firmly to hers, and I thrust my tongue into her mouth. Her hands slide around my waist, her chest molding to mine. And it's like we fit perfectly. Like our bodies were made for one another. It scares me, and I jolt backwards, our mouths disconnecting.

Exhaling, I turn from her. "I shouldn't have done that."

"Will you stop?" She shouts, frustration in her voice. "Stop feeling sorry for yourself. Stop acting like you don't deserve to be happy. Yes, your dad rejected you. Yes, he's gone now. But I'm not, damn it. I'm right here. And I'm not leaving, so you better figure this out."

I've never heard Emmy talk like this before, and honestly, it turns me on a little. Spinning around, I study her. In the moonlight her face is so pale it almost appears translucent. Her eyes are bright, her lips shimmering. When the wind kicks up, her hair swirls around her face, a few strands catching on her long eyelashes. Man, she's so beautiful that it makes me ache. The familiar longing spreads through my chest, cracking me wide open. As much as I want to deny her words, I know she's right.

I'm pulling away because I'm scared, but it is a cop-out. There's no way to protect myself forever. I am going to be hurt again. And I'll probably be rejected again. But that doesn't mean I need to close myself off to everyone who loves me. Emmy's here.

She always has been.

Even when I don't deserve it.

Even when I'm an ass.

So, why am I punishing her for what my dad's done?

"My heart chimes for you. Every hour on the hour," she says with a wink. "And sometimes even in between."

It's ridiculous, and cheesy, and such an Emmy thing to say.

And it's the final straw.

Stepping forward, I wrap my arms around her waist and tug her to me. "That was maybe the cheesiest thing I've ever heard."

"Eh, my mom's the writer. Not me." She smiles, her hands fluttering over my chest.

"What kind of ending do you think she'd

write for you and me?"

"One where you stop running," she says simply.

"Do you think that's possible for a guy like me?"

"I think anything's possible," she answers.

I nod, wanting desperately to believe her.

****

"Are you nervous about your first official game of the season tomorrow?" Emmy asks.

"No." Staring up at the black night sky, I reach for her hand, knotting our fingers together between us. We're lying on a blanket in the middle of the Prairie Creek Panthers baseball field. I wanted some time alone with my girl tonight. With the season approaching, I've been working hard and once the season starts, I'm only going to get busier. We discussed having a picnic out by the lake, but it's too cold, so we opted for the next best thing. The stadium lights are off, so it's dark except for the moonlight. Frankly, it's perfect.

"Really?" She sounds doubtful. "But you always get nervous before a game. I know Cal's super nervous. Not like he'll admit it, but I can tell."

She's right about Cal. I was with him earlier today and he was super intense. Of course he's always intense when it comes to baseball. And there's a lot riding on him this season. A lot riding on all of us actually. I was kind of surprised he didn't get upset with me when he found out I planned to go out with Emmy tonight. He said he was going to turn in early, get a good night's sleep. But he encouraged me to hang out with his sister.

In fact, his exact words were, "She helps you get your head on straight." Then he laughed, shaking his head. "Never thought Emmy would have a calming effect on anyone, but I guess she does."

Smiling at the memory, I roll my head to the side, studying Emmy's profile. "No reason for me to be nervous because I've got my good luck charm right here." Squeezing her hand, I flash her a grin. When she smiles back, I marvel at how far we've come. It seems crazy that a couple of weeks ago, I

374

was avoiding her. *Avoiding this*. Contentedness washes over me. With Emmy I feel a peace I've never experienced before. I feel whole. I feel accepted. I feel cared for. And it makes me feel like an idiot for trying to run from it.

Her face upturned, she stares at the sky.

"How many stars have you counted?" Hundreds of twinkling lights are splashed across the inky canvas. She's probably having a field day right now.

"One." Her neck swivels, her eyes catching mine.

I raise my brows. "One?"

She nods. "Yep. There's only one star I've been focused on tonight. It's the brightest one out here." Disconnecting our hands, she hoists herself up on one elbow, her gaze crashing into mine. "You."

My heart flips in my chest. I roll onto my side and reach for her. Curving my palm around her waist, I scoot her closer. Then I gently cover her lips with mine. After kissing her fruit scented lips softly, I draw back. "Thank you," I say.

"For what?"

"For not giving up on me."

"I'll never give up on you, Christian." Lifting her hand, she lightly touches my face. Her words are powerful, and her touch is healing. As her face nears mine, I know I'll be okay. Emmy is mending my broken heart one crack at a time. She's erasing my pain, stroke by stroke. And one day I know it will be gone for good.

EMMY

It smells like excitement.

It smells like fresh cut grass and leather baseball gloves.

It smells like popcorn and chips.

It smells like my childhood.

I've spent so many hours sitting in the stands during baseball games throughout my life, but I love it. I especially love the first game of the season. Nothing beats the buzz of anticipation, the energy radiating around me. Mom and Dad sit a few rows over, sharing a bag of kettle corn. I would sit with them, but I wanted to be in the first row. I wanted to be close to Christian. So close that he could glance over from where he crouches at home plate, and have a clear view of me cheering him on.

It's the first game I'm attending as his

girlfriend. The sentiment is not lost on me. For years I sat in the stands lusting after Christian. I'd watch him with rapt attention, knowing that he saw me as nothing more than his best friend's little sister. But now he saw me as so much more.

The game is about to start and my legs shake agitatedly. I find myself counting each bounce of my foot without even meaning to. One. Two. Three. I freeze, smelling her before seeing her. She always did wear too much perfume. I ignore Ashley as she passes me, and I don't have to see her face to know that it bothers her. She hates when people don't notice her. Being noticed is pretty much her only goal in life.

Out of the corner of my eye, I see her sit down a few feet from me. Pink flickers in my line of vision, but I keep my gaze trained forward. I'm not exactly surprised that she's here since she and Josh are still dating, but her presence does put a damper on things. Determined not to let her steal any of my joy, I search for Christian. When I catch a splash of his catcher's mask from the bullpen, my pulse quickens. And suddenly Ashley and her antics are a million miles away. Chris is all that matters to me right now.

"Hey, Emerson."

My head snaps up at the sound of Olivia's voice. She wears a flowing shirt, cut off shorts and Birkenstocks. Her hair is pinned back with bobby pins, and bracelets line her arms. Dan stands on the other side of her. I greet both of them, and then they take a seat next to me. Biting my lip, I return my attention to the field. I'm not sure how Christian will take Dan sitting with us, but I'm hoping he'll be okay with it.

Honestly, he seems to be accepting Olivia and Dan's relationship better than at first. The last couple of weeks he's softened a little toward Dan. I think it has a lot to do with the change in Olivia. She's happier now, not so sad or stressed. Not that Christian talks about it much. But I don't press him. Christian has always been a little guarded about his family issues, and I respect that. He'll open up when he's ready. Besides, I have an older brother. I know how out of touch guys are with their feelings. I don't expect Christian to blab on about his feelings like a girl.

The announcer begins talking, pulling me out of my internal thoughts. Olivia reaches over and squeezes my shoulder. I smile, the enthusiasm in the stands contagious. Sitting forward, I watch as the Prairie Creek Panthers take the field. Christian looks so hot in his uniform that my insides quiver. He glances over in my direction swiftly, and I swear I see the flicker of a smile before he takes his position behind home plate. I wish he'd given me more, but it's okay. I'll take it. I know how focused the guys get during a game. Any acknowledgment is huge.

Cal throws out his first pitch, and it sails past the batter, sliding seamlessly into Chris's glove. *First strike.* I smile. It's always amazing to watch Cal and Christian in action. Only someone who knows them well can see the silent signals they flash to each other, the unspoken language between them. But I see it, and it makes my heart swell. My boys. That's what they'll always be to me.

Since Christian and I started dating, the dynamic has changed. It's no longer Cal and Chris with me trailing behind. Now I'm more intricately involved. There are times when Christian and I want to be alone, but there are times I give them their space too. Either way, we're making it work, and Cal is coming around. He doesn't cringe or whine as often as he used to. We still can't kiss in front of him without him covering his eyes, but we can hold hands, even hug. *Baby steps.*

But no matter how we evolve and change over the years, one thing will remain the same. The bond they share, and the bond I share with them. They've always provided me protection, a safe place. They've been my confidantes, my mentors, my friends. And I know they always will be.

After that batter is struck out, another one approaches. I clap loudly, cheering on the boys, having no doubt the Prairie Creek Panthers will begin their winning streak today. This time the batter hits the ball, and it careens toward second base. Josh leaps for it, but it grazes his glove and lands in the grass. Cal shakes his head. I feel bad that the team didn't get the out, but a small part of me feels satisfaction that Josh bumbled the play and not Cal or Chris.

Josh kicks the dirt with his cleat, expletives pouring from his mouth. Dan sits forward, as if silently willing his son to get it together. Hayes shouts something out to Josh. I can't hear what he says, but knowing Hayes I'm sure it's encouraging. Chase and Nolan offer words of encouragement too, and Josh nods, his confidence returning.

Then to my right, Ashley hollers. "It's okay, baby."

I stiffen, knowing it's not the right thing to do. The girlfriend doesn't speak during the game. I learned that the hard way. Josh glances over, shooting daggers in her direction. Closing her mouth, she slumps in her seat. *Man, this game keeps getting better and better.*

Holding my breath, I watch the next batter step up to the plate. He's a big guy, his muscles bulging. As he swings the bat, I cringe. Clearly he's a hitter. Cal doesn't look fazed though, so I sit up straighter. The first pitch is a ball, and I wince.

C'mon, Cal.

The next one is a strike.

382

Here we go.

Chris and Cal have one of their silent conversations, and I sit up straight, waiting. Sure enough, two more strikes and that guy's outta here. Only one more out to go, and then we're up to bat. I find my shoulders relaxing a bit. *We've got this.*

After the next batter takes the plate, Cal fires a pitch. It looks good. And apparently it is, because the batter hits it straight up. I squint trying to see where it goes, only I don't see it at first. Then again, the sun's in my eyes. But Chris takes off, moving back toward the fence. Moving toward me. *Ah, it must be a foul.*

He sprints for the ball, holding out his arm and skidding in the dirt. I hop up, peering down at him. Then I let out a loud shriek when I see the white ball nestled in his brown glove. The stands erupt in cheers. When Christian stands, he holds up the glove, and his teammates holler. Then he throws off his catcher's mask and whirls around to face the stands.

My heart stops.

His gaze crashes into mine.

I freeze.

Stepping forward, he lifts his free arm and points at me. Then he curls his index finger toward himself, as if motioning me forward. I cock my head to the side, my lips curling a little. What is he doing? The entire place goes silent. My palms moisten, and my legs wobble. But I force myself to move forward like he's asking.

When I reach the fence, he says, "You're not gonna leave me hangin' in front of all these people, are you?"

"What?" I'm confused.

"I need a kiss from my girl."

My mouth goes dry, my body warming. I look around. "Won't you get in trouble?"

"Baby, I'm already in trouble. Don't make it for nothin'."

Giggling, I move closer. Wrapping my fingers around the cool metal, I angle my face toward Christian's through the fence. Leaning forward, I press my lips to his. I figure it will be a short kiss. A tiny peck. So I'm surprised when his tongue slips out, coaxing my lips open. I hold tighter to the fence in order to stay upright as our kiss deepens. It's amazing the affect Christian has on me. I know that I'm in front of a baseball stadium full of people, but for some reason it feels like it's just the two of us. Like we're the only two people in the world.

"Alcott, what the hell are you doing?" Coach Hopkins' voice rings out, jolting me back to reality. "This is a baseball game, not a scene from the Bachelor. Get over here!"

Chris draws his lips back. I blink as if I'm coming out of a daze.

"Emmy," Christian says softly, his fingers touching the edges of mine where they curl around the fence. "I love you." With a quick smile, he spins around and jogs toward his coach.

My head spins, and I feel dizzy. Did he say that he loves me?

"Wait!" I call after him. I can't let him leave after what he said. I need to tell him I feel the same way.

He cranes his neck.

"I love you too," I say.

385

"I know," he responds with a smile.

Stunned, I watch him as he follows his team into the dugout. My whole body heats up, sweat forming on my brow. I feel simultaneously embarrassed and giddy. Unhooking my fingers from the fence, I step away from it. When my gaze sweeps the stands, I am greeted with awed expressions. Expect for Ashley. She looks downright pissed.

Ignoring her, I walk unsteadily back to my seat. Lowering into it, I try not to look at Olivia. I know she loves me, but I'm not sure how she feels about me making out with her son in the middle of his baseball game. *Not exactly a moment for the scrapbook.* That reminds me that my parents are sitting a few rows up. Curling in on myself, I wish I could be like a turtle with the ability to hide in its shell. That would be useful right about now. Still, I don't regret what happened. It was the single most romantic moment of my life. And to top it off, Christian admitted that he loved me. That's huge.

It's more than huge.

It's everything I've ever wanted.

PLAY HARD (Make the Play #2) – Cal's story -
coming winter 2016!

Sign up for my newsletter to get release
information, exclusive giveaways, and insider
information: http://eepurl.com/sp8Q9

AUTHOR'S NOTE AND ACKNOWLEDGMENTS

The Playing for Keeps series was my first sports series. When the first book, FOR THE WIN, released almost a year ago, I wasn't sure how my readers would respond to it. But I was pleasantly surprised. Not only did my readers embrace it, but I gained many new readers. I found a whole new audience for my work – a readership hungry for sports romances. So after penning FOR THE SAVE, the last book in the Playing for Keeps series, I decided to keep writing in the sports romance genre.

I've always been a fan of small-town romances. I was once a big fan of shows like Dawson's Creek and One Tree Hill. So I decided to write a series centering around one high school baseball team set in a small town. At first I kicked around the idea of following one couple throughout the series, but the truth is I've never been good at that. I like to write spinoffs much more than I like to write actual series. As much as I love every couple I write about, I do get a little bored writing their story after awhile. I enjoy the rush of starting something new, of getting to know new characters. So in the end, I decided to write about a new couple in every book. Still the book is considered a series because the books will need to be read in order. And if you love Christian and Emmy, don't worry, they will be in the subsequent novels.

When I sat down to figure out the plot for this book, the first idea that came to mind was falling for the older brother's best friend. It's a premise I've always enjoyed reading about. I mean, what girl doesn't, right? And that's when Christian and Cal emerged. After I had them, I came up with the remaining characters on the team. The name Prairie Creek came from one of my readers - Ginelle Blanch - so thank you so much! After having that, I had the completed roster for the Prairie Creek Panthers. That's where the real Coach Hopkins came in. Both of my brothers are ball players. My brother Matt coaches and plays recreationally, and my brother Kagen is a professional pitcher. So I sent the roster to my brother Matt with stats on each character – age, weight, personality. Then he put them all into positions for me. This is when the story really came to life in my mind. I started to see the team, their dynamics, etc.

And that's when Emmy began talking in my head. Meeting Cal, Christian, Josh, Emmy and all of the other characters was such a fun experience. I really enjoyed writing their story and I hope you enjoyed reading it.

As always, I have many people to thank:

First, I have to thank the love of my life, Andrew. There were days where I struggled with this book. Days where I stared at the screen willing the characters to give me something – anything. On those days I would receive random texts from my husband saying things like, "You're amazing." "How did I get so lucky?" or "Miss you." And boom, I'd feel inspired again. Sorry, Christian, but you pale in comparison to the man who owns my heart.

Second, I have to thank my kids – Kayleen and Eli. They are constant inspirations to me. They encourage me, love me, and drive me nuts simultaneously. But I'm always blessed by their presence in my life. And I love them more than words can express.

Third, I have to thank those who helped me shape this book. They are as follows:

Matt and Kagen – your baseball knowledge is priceless.

Lisa Richardson – your editing skills are unmatched. So lucky to have you.

Megan Squires – Thank you for reading as I wrote and encouraging me along the way.

Susan Griscom – Thanks for beta reading.

Fan club – Your enthusiasm keeps me going.

Matt at the Cover Lure – Your cover is so perfect. I'm in love with it.

Beth Shelby – Thanks for being my blurb fairy.

And mostly, thank you to God. Everything I do is for you.

ABOUT THE AUTHOR

Amber Garza is the author of the bestselling *Playing for Keeps Series*, as well as many other bestselling young adult romance novels including *Tripping Me Up* and *The Summer We Fell*. She also has several new adult and adult romance novels including *Break Free*, *Star Struck* and *Head Above Water*. She has had a passion for the written word since she was a child making books out of notebook paper and staples. Her hobbies include reading and singing. Coffee and wine are her drinks of choice (not necessarily in that order). She writes while blaring music, and talks about her characters like they're real people. She currently lives in California with her amazing husband, and two hilarious children who provide her with enough material to keep her writing for years.